LP NYE
Nye, Nelson.
Bandido.

DATE DUE

12/20/6			

D1402184

BANDIDO

BANDIDO

NELSON NYE

THORNDIKE
CHIVERS

This Large Print edition is published by Thorndike Press, Waterville, Maine USA and by BBC Audiobooks Ltd, Bath, England.
Thorndike Press is an imprint of Thomson Gale, a part of The Thomson Corporation.
Thorndike is a trademark and used herein under license.

The text of this Large Print edition is unabridged.
Other aspects of the book may vary from the original edition.
Set in 16 pt. Plantin.

LIBRARY OF CONGRESS CATALOGING-IN-PUBLICATION DATA

Nye, Nelson C. (Nelson Coral), 1907–
    Bandido / by Nelson Nye.
        p. cm. — (Thorndike Press large print westerns.)
    ISBN 0-7862-8980-5 (lg. print : alk. paper)
    1. Large type books. I. Title.
PS3527.Y33B3 2006
813'.54—dc22   2006019221

BRITISH LIBRARY CATALOGUING-IN-PUBLICATION DATA AVAILABLE

Published in 2006 in the U.S. by arrangement with Golden West Literary Agency.
Published in 2007 in the U.K. by arrangement with Golden West Literary Agency.

U.K. Hardcover: 978 1 405 63930 9 (Chivers Large Print)
U.K. Softcover: 978 1 405 63931 6 (Camden Large Print)

Printed in the United States of America on permanent paper.
10 9 8 7 6 5 4 3 2 1

BANDIDO

1

Hours ago he had lost his horse in the mesquite-tangled roughs west of San Jon. He knew well enough now what a fool thing he'd done. Pulled up in the wind-blown black shadows of cedar, he stared with bitter eyes at the shaft of yellow light stabbing out of a shadeless window. It seemed fittingly ironic that having managed at last to find shelter, he was going to have to share it. A pity he couldn't have shared some of the luck which had dogged every turn he had made these last weeks.

Holding onto the branch he'd been about to push past he came the closest he had ever been to knowingly feeling sorry for himself. He sounded like a wind-broken bronc; he hadn't enough strength left to curse with. It was hole up here or be as certainly done as though that bunch had caught him.

He'd known the risk — was aware of it now, but no longer had any choice in the matter. If he didn't mighty soon get some help for his side, the slug might as well have gone where it had been aimed for. He didn't know how far behind they were or if he'd succeeded in losing them. He scrubbed hot cheeks with a brush-clawed hand and tried to think what fool things he might blab when fever got the best of him. Talk enough, probably, to hang him twice over. But it was out of his hands now.

He threw a look at the stars, at the wind-scuffed blackness pulsating around him, and shoved the branch out of his way. It took an unconscionable effort to push himself into movement. Then he was out in the perilous open, target of every shifting shadow. Wind swayed and shook him, snatching his breath away, fluttering and flapping loose ends of his clothing. Only stubbornness kept him going, stumbling, floundering over ground that wouldn't hold still for his feet.

He looked again for the window, could not find it. He'd been afraid of that light, but he was more afraid now. To have lost direction in thirty feet told more of his condition than a man could rightly stomach. He crashed into something, grappling it, desperately hanging on till half-numb hands discovered it was a side of the shack. He almost sobbed aloud in his relief, and this, too, told him something. It told how little time he had to use whatever sense was still in him.

He groped along the dark wall until one hand came against the rough planks of a door. It no longer mattered how much warning he gave, nor was there any good touching the gun at his hip. He was stuck with whatever he found here, so goddamn weak he couldn't even yell *boo!*

The door wasn't barred. The latch lifted easily. Some instinct turned him and his eyes picked out a pole corral in the gloom off to the left; and a horse there, catching his scent, lifted its head in a welcoming whinny. The man braced himself. When nothing further happened he looked again toward the horse, considering its possibilities. But that was no good either. With a disgusted scowl he pushed open the door.

The place was dark as the inside of a cow. He understood now what had happened to the light. Snuffed lampwick was unmistakable. He tried to locate the one who had put it out, but the only breathing he could hear was his own. The fellow may have slipped through the window; he might be standing with drawn gun behind the door. "Friend," the intruder said, "I need help."

"Scratch a match," the answer came.

The man in the doorway crazily laughed, but he didn't scratch anything. The hinges of his knees let go and the whole collapsed weight of him struck the floor.

When he next knew enough to understand what he was seeing, there was sun in the room, a great blinding blaze of it coming through the window. He judged it late afternoon, and above his face was a ceiling of planks laid over peeled poles that had cobwebs across them. He was flat on his back with no idea where he was or how he had got there until he saw the cowpuncher gear on the walls. Then his wits got to working and he tried to sit up, falling back with a groan as the room spun around.

He was lying there, sweating, when he heard steps outside. He pawed for his pistol and discovered he didn't even have belt or boots. He'd been peeled to his drawers, and the tightness that bound across his chest was a bandage. He remembered the girl.

Twisting his head he found her watching from the door. Her eyes, brightly green, were direct as a man's. Sorrel hair fanned out around her confident features, and the blue silk of the waist above the corduroy skirt showed plenty of conformation. "How do you feel?" she asked, coming into the room.

"You been here all night?" he said irritably as she bent over to fluff his pillow. The clean woman smell of her turned him self-conscious. He was glad when she stepped back.

"Hungry?"

He didn't know whether it was that or just a lone man's natural disquiet around a woman. He said gruffly, "You haven't answered my question."

She considered him a moment, and though he could not read her look he sensed she was amused about something. "Three nights — this will be the fourth," she nodded, smiling at the incredulity he showed.

Even then he realized she was a damned attractive number. She didn't seem in the least embarrassed, and this was something else that somehow bothered him. "Three nights!" he said, and alarm rushed through him. All kinds of avenues of thought opened up; he had to haul off and take a real hold on himself. *Three nights. . . .* He shook his head. The room didn't spin quite so dizzily this time. He touched the tight feel of the bandage. "Your work?"

Her eyes still smiled, but there were other things in them not so easily unraveled. "You

11

said you needed help."

"And you've been here all this time?"

"You were in no condition to be left alone."

He fingered the bandage, half scowling. "What about your people?" She said nothing to this and he eyed her more sharply. "Ain't they like to be getting upset — start a hunt for you?"

"I don't have any 'people'."

"You're no stray."

She laughed and got hold of a box and sat down. "You were lucky," she said. "Another inch to the left and you wouldn't have made it."

He felt suddenly whipped and there was wool in his ears. His head dropped back as the dizziness returned. A cool rag wiped sweat from his forehead. After that he must have dozed because the next thing he knew she had the box up beside him and a bowl in her hand.

He lost track of the hours. Twice when he awoke he was alone in the shack. Other times he recalled her being there with the bowl. He felt like a sick calf. His recollection was confused, patched with gaps and a muzzy vagueness through which he seemed to remember voices. "You've been out of your head," she told him.

12

"I'm not out of it now." He said after a moment, "There's something queer about this."

Her smile teased him. "Tomorrow," he said, "I'll pull out of here."

"You're weaker than you know."

"I'm not that weak!" He felt the dampness of his forehead, dragged the hand across his cheeks. They took on a little color, and by this she knew he realized she had shaved him. He said, "I guess there ain't much you don't know about me," and his lips tightened up. "You've done enough. I'm beholden. But there's a limit to how far a man can afford to go with a woman."

"There doesn't have to be, you know."

It was noon and the wide-open unshaded window put rich lights into the curves of her sorrel hair. The limit he had meant had been concerned with obligation, and the agility of mind introduced by her reply fetched a deepening awareness of the danger inherent here. Old hungers stirred as he considered her.

She was, he judged, in her middle twenties and obviously used to handling men as she pleased. The green eyes told him that. She had no rings on her fingers. There was pride in her face and confidence too, and a sensual curve to the provocative lips which

13

increased his disquiet. She dropped onto the box and lifted one knee six inches above the other and at arm's length clasped both hands about it. The green, still wisdom in her eyes disturbed him.

She said, apropos of nothing discernible, "Your gun went off while you were cleaning it, I suppose."

He felt the tightening of the skin about his mouth and tried to hide it. Finally managing a grin he hitched himself up until his back was against the wall. "When do I get my clothes?"

"You can probably sit up a while tomorrow." The corners of her eyes crinkled. "Are you in a terrible hurry?"

In the look he gave her she saw stubbornness and suspicion, more than a hint of bitterness. "You know enough about me to understand I'm running."

"I've suggested you don't have to be."

"We're getting nowhere fast."

She took the hands away from her knee and folded them in her lap and smiled. "A man could stay lost in this country for months. If he had the right connections."

"Turn the cards over."

"All right. I'm Tara Dow," she said, but it was plain this held no significance for him. The flatness of his stare remained unchanged until she said, "Of Bellfour."

That got home. Amusement tugged at the curve of her lips as she watched his shoulders come away from the wall. All the lines of his face broke apart as he cried: "Bellfour! You're connected with them?"

"I am Bellfour."

She was not prepared for the blaze of his eyes, for the irascible way he flung back the sheet and got up in one bound to stand white and trembling. He couldn't have looked more wild if she had called him a horse thief.

Loss of blood and shock caught up with him and he staggered, would have fallen had she not sensed this and leaped to catch him. He was heavier than he looked, and it took all her strength to get him back in the bunk. The knowledge that if he'd reached the floor she could never have managed it left her breathless.

She washed his bowl and the pan she'd cooked in and the crockery plate she had used herself, and all this while she felt him watching her. She dipped up the last of the water and held him while he drank thirstily. Then she took the pail and went after more, pausing en route to take care of the horses, trying to guess what had so upset him. She couldn't see anything about

Bellfour to do that. The very size of the outfit should have been reassurance. Nobody pushed Bellfour around.

She found his eyes closed and, after considering him, felt baffled. She went back out with towel and soap and took a bath in the creek, taking plenty of time to look over her thoughts. She dried her hair in the sun, afterwards brushing it with a currycomb she carried.

Next morning he said right after they'd eaten, "When do I get my clothes?"

She fetched his pants and boots and said, "I burned your shirt. You'll have to make out with this one."

"Would you mind clearing out while I get into these things?" he asked.

She picked up the dishes and took them out to the creek. When she came back he was sitting on the bunk looking gray and breathing hard. Her eyes went to the shirt. "With the sleeves rolled up that's a pretty fair fit. I see you found your gun."

His eyes were flat and hard again.

"Relax," she said. "What you need is rest. Your troubles aren't going to catch up with you here."

He looked at her then. "You're right about that. I'm pulling out after supper."

She put the dishes away and put the frypan into the cold oven of the stove. She came back, sat down on the box, and watched him curiously. "What's in your craw? Am I poison or something?" she asked.

His hands were groping in his pockets. "Your Durham," she said, "is over there in the cupboard." She watched him get up and move across the room to get it. He was recovering faster than any gunshot man she had ever run into. He was pale but he walked well enough. "There's whisky there too, if you think you could use some," she added.

He didn't touch the whisky, but came back with the makings and stood and rolled himself a smoke. "Matches back of the stove," she said, and watched him get and scratch one. *He's got the constitution of an ox,* she thought.

He blew smoke from his nose. "Who else knows about me being here?"

She started to speak but he cut in. "You've had help with me. You didn't get me into that bunk by yourself."

"One of the boys came by —"

He looked at her grimly. "This his shirt I've got on?"

"What difference . . ."

"Just like to know where I stand is all.

Man does what he has to do. That don't make him like it."

"He'll keep his mouth shut." She looked at the stiff still shape of him standing there, seeing the hardness that had been ground into him, considering the tight stubborn set of his features. She read temper, resentment, belligerence and, behind the bright blades of his eyes, the black desperation of a man driven too far.

He took a restless turn around the room and came back, still frowning. She'd seen a lot of men come through these hills and most of them carried the gunsmoke smell. They'd come off the Staked Plains with the law at their heels, and she'd no ground to believe this one was much different save perhaps in the degree and quality of his bitterness. You could tell by their eyes after you'd watched enough of them.

"I'm trying to help —"

"You've helped plenty."

He needed a haircut. His dark hair was thick, inclined to curl at the temples, and the wiry growth of his beard was like a blue shadow on his jowls already. Tomorrow he'd look like the rest of these saddletramps, but she knew he'd been a somebody once and still was in his own mind. The habit of command was in every gesture.

She'd done a lot of thinking about this fellow. "Bellfour," she said, "could use another hand."

He stubbed out the butt of his smoke and considered her. "Thought you said yesterday you were Bellfour."

"That's right."

"Bellfour is a syndicate." His voice was harsh. "The Bellfour Land & Cattle Company. Mail address, Six-shooter Siding."

"Well?"

He seemed to be finding it hard to reconcile her with such a development. The green eyes smiled. "What about it?"

"You the wife of the resident manager?"

She held up a hand.

"Some women when they're out of the house don't wear rings."

She laughed. "I would."

"His daughter then?"

She got up and said bluntly: "There is no one higher on Bellfour than myself. Not a wheel can be turned without my permission."

She saw the stubbornness come into his stare. He went over to the window, looking out without answering, finally coming back to sit down on the bunk. "How far are we from Texas?"

"The border? Forty miles," she answered.

"You wouldn't make a man walk all that way, would you?"

She grinned. "You're not trying to make Texas." The green eyes searched his face. "Why don't you get smart? They'll never catch you here."

"Sounds an awful long time the way you say it."

She came over to the bunk and stood looking down at him. His teeth shone against the tightened stretch of his lips. Her eyes narrowed in fresh appraisal, then moved openly over his face. "What are you hunting that's more important than security? Pride? Revenge? There is nothing the right man could not find in this country."

He shook his head.

"Bellfour," she cried, "is an empire! Sixty square miles and still growing!"

He pulled his booted feet up onto the bunk. "I once knew a man who had ten thousand head of cattle. At branding the tally showed a couple hundred short. Man turned out his whole crew and the rest disappeared while the hills were being searched." He lay back, stretching out, with his hands behind his head.

She said without smiling, "A good thing for you to remember."

"You don't need me."

"You better remember that, too."

2

Upgrade somewhere out of sight in the timber came the sound of running horses. She saw how the shock of this ran through him. He came onto his feet like a crouching cat.

She threw a hand out. "You won't need that gun. Bellfour —"

"I'm not working for Bellfour."

"You will be," she smiled, and went and stood in the door where the breeze touched her hair and pushed the thin folds of the skirt between her legs.

He heard the horses come over the ground, saw the dust. Tara Dow said, "What do I call you?" and a shout lifted out there, but the riders went on through the brush without stopping.

She felt the man's breath on the back of her neck. "Some of your outfit?"

She nodded. "They were paid last night. Tomorrow they'll come straggling back, most of them broke. Some won't be fit to work for a week — why is it men have to be such damned fools?"

"That dude in the calfskin vest," he said,

staring. "That your top screw?"

"No." She twisted around for a look at him. "That's Angel. Scurlock's the range boss." She looked briefly amused. "You'll be making his acquaintance when we get to headquarters."

He turned back after a bit and stretched out on the bunk. He was up again presently and this time went out and was gone a half hour. She saw him later at the corral looking over the horses, her own and the one she'd had Scurlock bring up for him — one that would give out in three miles if kicked into a hurry. She wasn't worried about him clearing out now. It was what he might try later that bothered her. There must be some way of pulling him into this.

They nooned off game she shot from the doorway.

"You can cook," he said, getting out the tobacco. She was pleased. It showed in the lift of her breasts, in the stillness that followed and the oblique way she eyed him. They considered each other with an increasing awareness.

She knew the power of her attraction; she also knew he had a mind filled with trouble. She hesitated, but time was running out and she let her full lips which had been rather sullenly together come apart in a smile.

Then, impatient with his restraint, she got up and came around the table.

She watched the curl of his smoke through the dance of the dust motes, and when he still didn't move let the upper fullness of one thigh settle against him. His glance came up and observed her carefully. The color in his face was stronger now, and the tip of her tongue crept past white teeth.

"I expect," he said, "we're going to have a dry summer."

She turned completely still. She began to tremble. The look she gave him would have withered white oak. She grabbed up a towel and her chunk of Pears' soap and set out for the creek as though the heel flies were after her. She spent almost two hours in the water before she came back, still seething.

By the time she got supper onto the table she seemed — if she had not forgiven him — at least to have reached some kind of truce with herself. She even managed a brittle smile when he pulled out and held the chair for her.

The meal was a quiet one, neither of them able to indulge in small talk. When she put down her fork he excused himself and went outside. A frog-shaped butte rose above the brush behind the pole corral. By dint of much effort and several pauses for rest he managed to get onto the rock's exposed shoulders. From this vantage a considerable view opened up in the direction of Texas. South, a line of bluffs concealed whatever lay beyond them and north, lavenderish with distance, a mountain showed and not much else. Timber cut off all sight of the west. Bellfour headquarters would be off that way. He didn't see much hope of avoiding it though he had no intention of remaining. Let her think what she wanted. He'd gone over this and over it and he'd pull out the first chance he had.

He was not a free agent. He wasn't even an outlaw in the generally accepted sense of the term. He was a syndicate victim, a goddamn chump who'd let a banker make a fool of him.

Quite a number of Texas ranchers in the last several years had been experimenting with Shorthorns. But Howisgrenn, the banker, couldn't abide hearsay evidence and never trusted figures he had not put together himself — Matt Tretisson had heard this all of his life. So when Howisgrenn approached him after Matt's father died, there had been no reason for Matt to walk wide of him. For years the bank had carried Tretisson paper and Matt, just back from college, reckoned when he saw the banker driving into the yard he'd probably come for an accounting. Civilities exchanged, Matt put it to him bluntly.

"Well no," Howisgrenn said, and showed his dry grin. "I'm not worrying about you, Matt. Understand you've been studying animal husbandry. What's your opinion of these newfangled Shorthorns?"

"They're a good beef cattle."

"Think they could be raised in this country?"

"I don't see why not." Matt went into the matter with him.

Howisgrenn pursed his mouth thoughtfully. "Going to take a while though to find out the real straight of it. Ever think of trying them yourself?"

Matt had said with a laugh, "This spread isn't equipped for that kind of experiment. I'd have to have more water. I'd have to put in better grasses."

"You'd have to fence," Howisgrenn nodded. "But a man wouldn't need so much acreage — that's one of the arguments for 'em, ain't it?"

Matt said, "Yes. Less ground, less handling. More and better beef."

"There's a place . . ."

"I haven't got that kind of money."

"We can take care of that," Howisgrenn

smiled, "if you're willing to gamble. We'd have to take in this ranch, but you could pick up the Oaks place which ought to be about right. I'll carry the difference on the books and we'll advance you enough for the wire, foundation stock and miscellaneous overhead. Want to try it?"

The idea had fired Matt's imagination. He'd been younger then, filled with enthusiasim, impressed that a banker could show so much faith in him. "You'll be putting your education to work," Howisgrenn said. "It's not just you I'll be helping; I want this country to grow. You'll be gambling your time and supplying the elbow grease. Folks will call you a fool and you'll have plenty of headaches but with any kind of luck — if you're right about these cattle — you'll pay out in ten years. You'll be a big man around here."

Few kids in Matt's shoes would have turned the deal down. He took a week to look it over before he signed papers. It took three months of backbreaking work to get the new place ready. He'd told his dad's crew he'd keep every man who wanted to come with him; he wound up with three. The older hands, quitting, shook their heads like he was crazy. "You're goin' in over your nose," they advised him. "Them hothouse cows won't do no good here." He hired other men to take their places until he could know how many he'd need, and was the proudest man in Texas the day they put the new stock in fenced pastures. People came from all over to find out what he'd gone into. A few went away with queer looks in their eyes, but the most of them shook their heads, scowling darkly.

In spite of the headaches and losses he'd prospered. As the years rolled around and the calf crops became more obviously profitable some of his neighbors came to Matt for advice. Some of them actually invested, buying seed stock, and people came from far places to study his program. It made a lot of believers.

After selling his surplus at the end of the ninth year Matt was one of the most talked-about men in West Texas. He was judged to be worth close to two hundred thousand which, of course, was considerably exaggerated. Nevertheless he'd done well. The venture had more than paid its own way, and though he'd put most of the profit back into the operation he'd held out enough to stay even at the bank. The whole deal was still mortgaged for the amount of the loan, but his total indebtedness was less than five thousand which he could have paid off had

Howisgrenn not discouraged this.

How sharply it all came back, even now! He'd gone in after he'd gotten the beef money last year determined to put himself out of the red. Howisgrenn had got out the bottle of Four Star and they'd had a couple of drinks. "I'm going to write you a check," Matt had said, "and get out of your clutches once and for all."

"I'd rather have you on the books. That way," Howisgrenn smiled, "I can feel important when I hear folks talking about that fellow Tretisson." He looked at Matt, sobering. "What's the rub?"

"Call me superstitious," Matt said, "but get out that last note and the mortgage you're holding. I want to see you stamp them PAID."

"Thought I agreed to carry you ten years. If I'm not worrying I can't see why you should. If that cattle check's burning a hole in your account . . ."

"It's getting so I can't sleep any more. Every last nickel I owe is secured by that mortgage," Matt said, taking a cigar from the box Howisgrenn offered. "Supposing —"

"Supposing is a fool's game."

"Maybe so, but I would feel a lot better . . ."

"Have I ever steered you wrong?"

In all honesty Matt had to shake his head.

"Then don't be a chump. Keep your money working. You've been wanting to try one of those Ken Freer bulls. Fellow named Cramwonger east of Lubbock is just about ready to let go of his herd sire — I talked yesterday to a party that's been trying to make a deal for him. They're five hundred dollars apart on the price. You toss twenty-eight hundred into Cramwonger's lap . . ."

In the end Matt talked himself into it. He had seen that bull and went and looked at him again. He looked at some of the calves, pictured what this cross would do, and wound up taking the old fellow home with him.

Never in his life had Matt put in such a winter. Six days hand-running they found cut wire. His losses were not heavy but with that mortgage hanging over him Matt put the whole crew to riding fence. He was clever about this, shifting patrols and personnel, steering away from any semblance of a pattern. The wire cutting stopped, but tempers turned short.

In the middle of January, with a storm coming up, the big stack in pasture ten caught fire. With all hands fetched to fight it two others showed flame at opposite ends of the ranch and the wind-whipped stench of coal oil could be smelled a mile away.

In the morning it was snowing hard. Seventy yards of fence were down, almost a hundred head of three-year-olds missing, and three big stacks gone up in smoke. It was a staggering blow and, to make bad worse, the stock had been taken before the storm struck. There were no tracks to follow, no clues at all.

Hay, when Matt inquired, appeared to have become uncommonly scarce. He had to borrow from the bank to replace the amount he'd lost at a price that had doubled from what it was before the storm. They had a good man for sheriff; he put on extra deputies and scoured the county from end to end, but Matt's cattle were never found.

He worked furiously all spring, in the saddle from dawn to dark and sometimes through half the night as well. He borrowed again to put on more men, and though that damned old bull got some first-rate calves he was a long way short of getting the numbers Matt had looked for. He proved a shy breeder and Matt was really feeling the loss. To meet his notes at the bank he had to convert stock to cash, and the loss of those stolen three-year-olds forced him to dip into cattle saved for breeding. He borrowed another six thousand to advertise a sale and he got a man from Dallas who could "talk lard off a gnit" but his line didn't stir up the crowd that came to the sale. They were shoppers not buyers, and every animal chosen cost Matt dearly.

He cleared enough to take care of his notes but nothing at all toward that final last payment. He went in to see Howisgrenn. The man cleared the notes but pulled a long face when Matt mentioned the mortgage. "Been a bad winter, Matt. Don't see how I can help you."

Matt stared at him unbelievingly.

"You claiming you can't give me any more time?"

"I'm afraid," Howisgrenn said, "that's the size of it." The banker refused to meet Matt's stare. He played with a blotter.

"God damn it," Matt shouted, "you can't do this to me!"

Howisgrenn said wearily, "The bank's got some bad paper. The examiner's due; the directors are squawking. They've figured your place to make good on our losses. My hands are tied, Tretisson."

"I'll talk to 'em! Henshaw and Gaines —"

Howisgrenn shook his head. "They're not on the Board now." He mumbled the names of the bank's present bosses. Matt Tretisson said bitterly, "The Quitaque Pool — that highbinding syndicate that's gobbled everything from Big Spring to Childress! Why, they're worse'n a plague of locusts —"

He heard a door open in back of him. A clerk's voice said, "A Mr. Quares to see you, sir," and Howisgrenn threw out his hands. "We'll have to drop this for now. Believe me, Tretisson, if there was . . ."

Matt's anger, as he continued to stare at the banker, gave way to deep loathing. Sick and disgusted he turned and stumbled out.

He found his horse and got aboard and for three hours rode in a state of shock before his mind cleared enough for him to notice his surroundings. He was on the road to Henshaw's, a fifty-mile ride; and, since he'd already come about a third of the way, he decided to keep on. There wasn't much chance the man would help him, but as one of the region's big ranchers Henshaw would be as likely as anyone to know of someone who could.

He stopped overnight with a squatter and didn't miss his pistol until he was getting ready for bed. He remembered then he had left it on his saddle when he went into the bank. Some barfly had probably taken it. A sign of the times, he thought bitterly. It was a wonder they hadn't made off with his horse!

He got to Big H the next day and found Henshaw supervising the gentling of a racy-looking two-year-old Morgan. The rancher saw him and waved and got down off the corral. "Matt, how are you?" he said, shaking hands. "How'd the sale go?"

Matt told him. Henshaw said, "That figures. Let's get out of this heat." They walked over to the house and went into his office where he got out a bottle and a couple of glasses. "You've got that syndicate to thank. The word went around to lay off of your stuff."

Matt stared at him grimly. "They've got that much influence?"

"You heard about me getting froze out of the bank?"

"Howisgrenn mentioned you weren't on the Board."

"He ought to know!" Henshaw's eyes were black with anger. "Bank had some notes the Pool wanted to get hold of — I didn't find out about that till later." He said, growling: "They had some kind of reorganization. Howisgrenn jobbed us. When the stock was reshuffled Gaines and me was out — they made a deal, I think, and took him into the Pool. That banker, I mean."

Matt frowned a while in silence. He finally told Henshaw what he'd learned at the bank.

The rancher nodded. "It figures. I'd help you," he said, "but I can't lay hold of that much. If I was to turn in my stock — this new stuff's nontransferrable — they'd hold up the payoff till it was too late to matter. Can't see nobody else helpin' you, either — not with that Pool breathing down your neck. Ain't a thing you can do. Doubt if you'll be able even to unload your equity."

All the way back to town Matt kept turning it over, hunting an out. He didn't stop on this trip; he'd got a fresh mount from Henshaw and rode straight through. In the cold gray hour that comes just before dawn he pulled up at Fenastair's livery and, when the old man came out rubbing sleep from his face, said, "Put this hull on another horse, will you?" In the smoky light from the overhead lantern the liveryman's eyes looked like holes in a blanket.

His mouth shaped words but couldn't get any sound in them. He began to shake and then he grabbed Matt's arm and pulled him into the shadows. "Are ye daft, mon?"

Matt sniffed of the old man's breath and shook his head, not getting this. "I'm going to need a fresh mount. . . ."

"Take what you want but dinna be tellin'
me. An' don't go oot to the ranch, laddie."

Matt eyed the damp shine of the liveryman's cheeks. Never except under extreme
provocation did the burr of the Scots get
into his talk. Fenastair's nervous glance
swept the gloom. Before Matt could put any
questions the man hauled him over to the
wall by the lantern. A broadside was there,
the words leaping out at him. WANTED —
Dead or Alive! $1,000 REWARD *will be paid
for information leading to the arrest or ap-
prehension of* MATT TRETISSON, *sought in
connection with the murder of Alvis Blacley
. . .*

Blacley was chief clerk at the bank. With
his gut in a twist Matt read how, in a fit of
black rage brought on by the bank's refusal
to extend the bad risk of his loan any
further, he had two days ago in Howisgrenn's office flashed a gun in the man's
face just as Blacley had come in with a client. The gun had gone off, Blacley had collapsed. Tretisson had fled to a horse tied
outside and gotten clear.

"That's a goddamn lie!"

The liveryman paled, stepping back, his
eyes watchful.

"Some would hae thought so but ye can't
blink the gun, lad, an' ye canna get rid of

the corpus."

It seemed that Howisgrenn, trying to cover up for Matt, had declared the shooting an accident. Matt, according to the banker, had been remarkably upset and excited. By this version Blacley had lost his head and jumped Matt, the gun going off in the resultant struggle; but the client — Cid Quares, a stranger to these parts — had told a different story. Quares had testified Tretisson had given every indication of being about to shoot Howisgrenn, that Blacley had jumped between them and caught the bullet intended for the banker. Tretisson, suddenly realizing the enormity of what he had done — understandably horrified — had dropped the gun and bolted.

" 'Tis yer own pistol, Matthew."

Of course it was his pistol! *How else could they have framed him?* He still remembered the broomstick thinness of the liveryman's arm, how his fingers had dug into it, how the man's face had twisted. Even now he could hear himself saying stupidly, "They believed it?" and knew he would have too had it been someone else that stranger had put the finger on.

He'd no idea how long he stood. He remembered Fenastair coming up with a horse, thrusting the reins in his hands and helping him on it — of roosters crowing as he rode out of town. The rest was a nightmare of riding and hiding, knowing if he were caught he hadn't a Mexican's chance of ever coming to trial. This was what a syndicate had done to him, the Quitaque Pool through power and pressure, through the cupidity and treachery of a county seat banker.

He remembered how it had worked through his blood, spreading its poison through every corner of his mind, feeding on hate, gnawing away his judgment until in his terrible anger all he'd found room for in his black thoughts was vengeance.

It didn't seem possible he could have been such a fool as to leap from the frying pan into the fire, yet this was what he had done. He could see that now in the bitterness of hindsight. All he had been able to think of then was how cold-bloodedly that bunch had framed him, talking him into being their guinea pig, into proving the profit that could be made out of purebreds, doing him out of ten years of his life and then doing him out of all the fruits of that labor — stealing him blind and then putting the law on him. The time and thought they had put into it, studying his habits, then triggering the trap with his own gun! Even Howisgrenn's mention of Henshaw and Gaines had been deliberate bait to get him onto a horse while they clinched the case against him. Henshaw could talk himself blue in the face — that homesteader, too, without improving Matt's position. The Pool had no intention of affording him a chance for shooting off his jaw. They had made their point. DEAD OR ALIVE. And a bounty to insure it!

Tretisson wiped the cold sweat from his cheeks. He'd played right into their hands with his anger. He had wanted to hurt them — and maybe he had, but he had hurt himself more in the final accounting, for he had conformed to the pattern they had forecast and built for him. He had banded together a handful of hard-cases, fly-by-night grifters, and raided the ranch, burning the buildings, running off cattle. They had robbed the bank and dug for the tules with a hundred thousand dollars.

Matt was still packing it after the breakup, but it was not on the horse the posse had shot from under him. He had taken enough time to bury it and this was how they had come so near to catching him. Matt's bunch were to rendezvous at Sixshooter Siding, well outside the lawful reach of stars from Texas. With time running through his fingers Matt wasn't at all sure he wanted to rejoin his partners. He hadn't come to any decision, but he was beginning to wonder how much he understood of what he knew about those fellows.

He looked off again toward Texas, seeing how the country had deepened to blues and purples, discovering no dust which might have been thrown up by horsemen. A wild country — he could give the girl that. He got up, gingerly turning himself, and looked for the best way down. Howisgrenn had been right about one thing. Matt had certainly grown up to cut one hell of a splash! One hundred thousand dollars worth. He reckoned the price on his pelt had gone up and wondered if Tara had her eye on it.

By the time he got down off the rock he was tired enough to rest. His mind conjured up again the look of those fellows who were expecting to help him get rid of the spoils, and he supposed, if he had to, he could ride a ways tonight. But it wouldn't be smart. Considering the shape he was in and Tara. . . . No, he decided, it wouldn't be at all smart.

He was smoking, absent-mindedly scratching the ears of the old horse, when she came out and moved up to lean against the poles. "Kind of awkward," she said, "to converse with a man for whom one hasn't any handle."

"Call me Calico," he smiled, glancing down at the borrowed shirt.

Her eyes went over him, cool as mountain water. "When a man's on the dodge one name's as good as another, I guess," she said with more indifference than he'd expected her to manage.

He massaged the gelding's withers and wondered how much she'd found out about him. She said abruptly: "If you're shining up to those nags in the hope of making off on one you're wasting your time."

He glanced around with a chuckle. "You don't miss much."

"You're not the first of your kind that ever came through these hills."

"You got the rest of them on Bellfour?"

She said, "Is it women in general you don't like or just me?"

3

How did a man go about telling a woman he'd a flock of prior commitments? She had probably saved his life. She didn't look the sort to lose her head over any man, yet she had gone out of her way on his behalf, made it plain she was ready to go further. A lot of woman — but what did she want of him? Was it all on the surface, a simple matter of physical attraction, or was she up to some darker game? His experience with Howisgrenn could be steering him wrong but, short of proof to the contrary, he had no intention of changing his mind. He had his own life to live. Let her think what she wanted.

She was watching him closely. "If I were to turn you loose with a horse, where would you head for?"

"That what you're figuring to do?"

Her eyes told him nothing. "Might be a good thing for me if I did, but it wouldn't be doing you much of a favor. Country's all Greek to you. It may be equally strange to whoever is hunting you, but they can probably find help who will know every inch of it. . . . Outside Bellfour."

No getting around that. Her mind dug straight to the core of a problem, wasting no time with the outer looks of a thing. This got Matt's grudging admiration. It also put his guard up.

"You've a good thing here," she said. "Stay with it." She turned with a flutter of skirts and departed.

It was dark when he followed, and he still hadn't figured her. She was asleep in the chair with a blanket thrown over her. He got into the bunk as he was and spent a bleak while trying to add up the angles. He finally pulled off his boots and, unbuckling his cartridge belt, reached these things down to the floor where they'd be handy. After a while he gave out to be snoring.

He saw Tara open her eyes. She watched him for twenty minutes before she put back the blanket and slipped barefoot into the moonlit night.

After breakfast she looked at his wound and rebandaged it. "When do we ride?" he asked, buttoning the shirt up.

"You feel up to it?"

"I could make out to manage if we don't go too far."

"Four miles," she said. "Perhaps we'll try it tomorrow."

Something told him she was lying and he remembered last night. She hadn't slipped out to go grunt in the three-holer. She baffled him and worried him. An uneasy tension had taken hold of this room.

She went over to the bunk and made up his blankets.

Four of the crew went past in midmorning, homeward bound; none of them stopped. None of them appeared even to notice the shack or the pair of penned horses their own mounts nickered back at. In some odd angering way this disquieted him.

As she had said, Bellfour was an empire. Perhaps she wasn't to be judged in a class with other women. Sixty square miles was considerable territory even in New Mexico. The very nature of her position in the hierarchy of this range, the lonely isolation, enforced companionship of men. . . . What the hell was he hunting excuses for? If she was minded to make a few rules of her own, who was he to say this was not her privilege?

After she'd cleared away the debris of their nooning, another horsebacker went clip-clopping past. Tretisson borrowed the razor and scraped at his whiskers, aware of her puzzled interest. Some of the driven look went out of her face. "Could it be you're figuring to stay a while?"

He grinned at her reflection.

Her eyes, green as new grass, continued to regard him unblinkingly. She was deep, all right. A man would have to watch his step.

He cleaned the razor and put it away. Why in God's name should he try to understand her! She was obviously capricious — what the hell difference did it make to him? He'd be getting clean out of this deal quick as could be. But not, he thought darkly, if she had her way. Behind the things she'd shoved out for him to look at, what was she really? Bold, impulsive, rash, conniving or just another female who didn't know her own mind?

Her glance had dropped to his waist. "You any good with that gun?"

"I could probably make out to hit the side of a barn."

"I'll bet," she said, and got up and went out.

He was more disturbed than he was willing to admit. She didn't look like one who'd talk to hear her jaw rattle. She wasn't the kind — or was she? Damned little she had said made any sense when you came right down to it. And yet in another way it did. If she were determined to keep him tied to her apronstrings . . .

Scowling he took out the pistol and checked it. Being alone with her here was not good for a man. Particularly it was not good for any gunshot fool who'd come out of the blue. She could add two and two, and she could probably get four. There were angles to this thing which definitely alarmed him. She could, if she were minded, consider herself compromised. And make a good case of it.

She was presently back, hunting soap and a towel. She was the bathingest woman . . . He looked at her slanchways. "This is the flossiest linecamp I ever put up at. Sheets on the bunk, by God — even a pillow. Turkish towels to wipe a guy's mug with!"

She got out the makings and put together a smoke. She saw that he was shocked, and she showed a scornful amusement. "We try to keep our boys happy." She pulled off her boots and wriggled bare feet looking up at him.

He didn't miss the look. He tried to play dumb, ignoring it. "Any chance of me sponging off while you're swimming?"

"Creek won't care. It's plenty big enough for both of us."

The green eyes laughed when heat crept into his cheeks. "If I hadn't seen the blood myself I'd swear your veins were filled with pap. I don't think," she said, putting a match to her coffin nail, "I've ever come across your kind before."

He could have told her that went double. He stared at the smoke curling out of her nose and felt half sick with the sight of it. When she was done she stubbed out the butt, caught up the bucket and came back with it brimming. She put it down just inside the door, took her towel and soap and departed.

Matt unbuckled his shell belt. "Were you wanting me to shoot a couple fish for our supper?"

She paused to look back at him. "Just wondering," she said, "if you could make out to take care of yourself."

He thought about that all the time he was washing.

She hadn't been kidding. He remembered that first night, the remembered mutter of voices. She'd come out to this shack to meet somebody, and it was plain enough she had not been stood up. If she'd gotten this shirt from him it would probably be recognized.

Wherever a woman had the say with an outfit, there you could look to find things in an uproar. Preferential treatment, resentment and jealousy. Was this what she'd meant — that she couldn't control them?

He couldn't see her admitting it.

She certainly aimed to get something out of him. So far he'd sidestepped her bait, but her pride would never leave it there. It would keep poking and picking at the flaws she found in him until it finally discovered some way to constrain him.

She could be in a mood to welcome trouble. Some of her crew weren't going to like the idea of her being out here alone with him. Thing like that could get a man killed. . . . Was that what she wanted, to get someone killed?

Dusk was chasing its blues through the shadows when Tretisson next heard the approach of hoofs. In the corral both horses nickered and were answered, horsemen presently appearing in the brush. Pride, Matt remembered, could be a terrible thing. He got a hand around his pistol, altering the cant of the holster, and the riders pulled up with a jingle of bit chains. There seemed to be five, and he was not sure they saw him. Then Tara, without speaking, got up and went in. A match, flaring, went to the wick of a lamp. Light sprang out of all the shack's openings.

Saddle leather skreaked and a man got down. By the calfskin vest Matt placed him as Angel. He came into the rectangle of light from the door, clean shaven and compact. He moved as though his boots walked on springs.

He wasn't old. He wasn't ugly. About average in height but something in the way he carried himself made him appear taller than his actual inches. Here, Matt guessed, was one of the privileged ones.

Tara came out doing something to her

hair. Angel, stiffening, stared, and his glance jerked around to stab at Matt in the shadows.

Something wicked came into the feel of this thing. Matt knew there'd been no reason for the girl to touch her hair — certainly not the one Angel had drawn from it. There had been no need for her to light that lamp.

Sweat slicked the grip of his pistol. The fellow's face was bland, even oddly cherubic, the small ears almost hidden in the rumpled gleam of blond curls. He didn't look riled, but a centipede doesn't until he's dug his hooks in.

"We'll go back with you," Tara said, coolly brisk. "Have one of the boys throw the hulls on those horses."

Angel stood in his fifty-dollar boots, gently rocking. "We got enough strays on Bellfour now."

"We could always weed a few out," she said.

Matt saw the two guns as the man wheeled to face her. His smug assurance had torn, and he stood there looking filled with his temper. He was a man who'd trained speed to the dexterity of gunplay, who had got so used to counting on this he could not think his way past a thing suddenly blocking it.

His stare picked up Matt. The whole look of him brightened. "Get out here where we can see what we're dealin' with!"

Matt considered. It was pride pulled him up. The girl had outfigured him. Moving into the light he felt the weight of their inspection. He watched Angel's stare fasten onto the shirt and heard the breath he pulled into him. Someone back of the man swore.

There were forces working here beyond Matt's comprehension, but he gathered from the frozen-faced way they all stared, this much of the crew would take their orders from Angel. The strengthening pressures around him warned Matt how tight a bind this was, and a growing sense of wildness got into him. Had he been right about the girl? Was it a killing she had rigged this for? Or had she simply been hunting an extra gun, seeking to bind it with ties more enduring than the monetary ones which presumably held these others?

He gave the gun fighter his full attention, sensing the man's distrust, the bright suspicion that was riding him. There were sparks swirling deep in his outraged stare. The shirt was turning him crazy just as the matador's cape, or muleta, flourished before its face infuriates the bull. In this moment of truth

Matt Tretisson, electrified, knew the girl was afraid of this gun fighter.

There was in Angel's look the frenzy of a man who sees another walking off with something counted for his own. In a flash of intuition the whole scope and desperate turn of this was beginning to make sense to Matt.

Bellfour had been built with the guns of these saddle bums. Using herself as bait she had held them in line, playing each against the other until she found which two were strongest — Angel, apparently, and the one she'd got this shirt from, the one she'd slipped off to this cabin to meet. But something she had not allowed for had happened, and trapped — certainly frightened — she had tried to pull Matt in. When other things failed she'd put him into this shirt, knowing what the sight of it would do to the gun fighter, probably hoping Matt would kill him.

No time for regrets. Angel was coming, both spread-fingered hands crouched above his pistols. Matt's stomach knotted, then his voice lashed out. "If you want trouble with me," he said, "you can get it," and, instead of retreating, stepped into the man. He threw blurred fists into the gun fighter's middle, smashing a knee into that jackknifing face. The man cried out, got hung up in his spurs, lost his balance and fell.

Matt's stare raked the others. The audacity of his attack, his complete uncaringness in the face of their numbers, held them rooted.

Angel picked himself out of the dust, breathing hard. There was blood on his chin. His eyes were unfocused. Matt's voice hit out with a warning flatness: "You go for those guns and they'll bury you here."

Angel's eyes, wild now, found him. Matt cracked a hand against the side of his mouth. Again the gun fighter stumbled but he kept on his feet and, backing out of Matt's reach, stood like a chained tiger.

He looked murderous — visibly shaking with his fury and with the need to retaliate. Yet he stood, held against his will by something strongly felt.

Matt couldn't take much more of this. He had to hammer it home before the man got his back up. "You heard her," he said. "Go tend to those horses."

Angel's eyes were like glass. His bloody mouth twitched. With a strangled cry he plunged into the dark.

4

They rode without talk.

An orange moon showed through the tree branches, climbed higher and brightened. They moved out of the blackness of the roundabout timber, picking a precarious way across the shale of a slope all blue and silver. Yellow grass came underfoot, and by this Matt knew the land had been some time without rain. A long silence enfolded this country broken only by the hoofs of their walking horses. Tara Dow rode up ahead, the rest of them behind him — all, that is, but the two-gun man. Matt hadn't seen Angel since he'd quit the cabin.

Nothing had been solved. The world wasn't big enough for both of them. It was like Matt's past — temporarily shelved but not forgotten. It would be coming up again, would have to be settled.

His thoughts slipped away to the men who had helped him sack Howisgrenn's bank — Gurd Pace and those others — and a deeper unrest came into his look. There was always a hereafter until the ground rattled down on you.

Now the way leveled off and Tara's voice called him up to her. All the coolness had gone out of her. She said fiercely, defiantly almost, "I've had to fight fire with fire to hold onto this."

Matt said, "People do what they have to do — what they think they have to anyway."

He thought she looked at him queerly. She was near enough to touch if he had put out a hand. He felt the stir of long hungers. These had nothing to do with the kind of person she was, only with the physical her that was so close to him. He didn't have to understand. Desire was an urge that came out of the blood, and there was no good picking the skin and bones of it to pieces. Tara Dow could be the end and the beginning of all the dreams he'd ever worked for, all the warmth and light and headlong passion that shaped a man's hopes and gave his being purpose. But he kept remembering the shirt.

She said, "I can't believe you're as disillusioned as you seem. You're not like these others —"

"No one compelled you to hire them."

"You don't know what I've been up against."

"They're not much, I'd say, to lean on."

"They're insurance," she said sharply, "against people who would tear Bellfour apart!"

"Gun rowdies. Riffraff run out of better places."

"They know where they stand. If they quit me they've got to run. They know how far they'd get trying that. I can trust them."

"Then why are you trying to drag me into it?"

"You didn't have to strike Angel."

"No," he said bitterly, "I could have let the son of a bitch shoot me." Her chin stiffened up and she stared straight in front of her. He considered the side of her face and said harshly, "Angel recognized that shirt. You aimed for him to, knowing what it would do to him!"

She cut her horse with the quirt, then swerved back to say angrily: "Do you apply that yardstick to the things *you* have done?"

"I'm not judging you —"

"You think when I gave you that shirt I was trying to get you killed?"

"I think you figured to get somebody killed."

"Maybe I did — I had plenty of reason!"

He rode on without answering, her words tramping through him. He guessed she probably had. He had found plenty of reason for hitting Howisgrenn's bank, but that hadn't made him any less of a fool. Like himself she had burned her bridges behind her. She could do nothing now, like himself, but face it.

He said finally into the uncomfortable quiet, "You were playing them against each other to hang onto your control. What happens to it now?"

He saw the tautness of her mouth, the stubborn glint of her angry eyes. "You know what will probably happen," he said. "They won't both get killed. What kind of a club will you hold over the other?"

"I'll take care of it," she said, and kicked her horse into a lope.

He made no attempt to stay up with her. The ride was hard enough on him jogging along as he was. They were swinging back toward the creek which had crescented here. Beside the line of ragged willows he saw her pull up to wait. He glanced back. Angel's men were warily keeping their distance, rifles across saddlebows.

He had no intention of testing their marksmanship. He'd go on to Bellfour and there be guided by developments. One thing he was sure of. He'd not get into another bind if he could help it.

His wound was hurting again. The bandage felt dry. Tara said when he came up with her, "Sometimes I think I can't stand this country!" Surprised by her vehemence he watched her twist around in the saddle for a look at those others. She brought her glance back. "You wrench your side in that scuffle?"

"I'll make out," Tretisson said. Beyond her the water was churning up a white froth. The creek was wider here and shallow. She said, "It's the Tucumcari." He could see the wet glisten of stones.

"What's the matter with the country? Don't you own a big slab of it?"

"Sometimes," she said, "I think it owns me. You don't know what it's like to be a woman on a place the size of Bellfour, taxed with its decisions, damned if you do and considered a fool if you don't. The worst of it, to me, is knowing people are always watching, picking you to pieces while they bow and scrape, ready to take advantage of the least sign of weakness." She said on a rising note of resentment, "No wonder I'm hard. I have to be hard or there would be nothing left!"

Matt said of the others, "Those birds aren't coming up till we get moving."

She turned her horse; and across the creek where trees loomed darkest a sound of metal came off rock. Both the girl and Tretisson wheeled, darkly nervous. Tara said tightly, "There's somebody over there."

"That fellow whose shirt I've got on," he said, "maybe."

Her shoulders moved. "It might be Angel. . . ."

"What do you want me to do — throw a shot at him?"

She had her own anger; he saw it rush into her face as she twisted. "Isn't there any faith left at all in you!"

She had depths of fury he had not guessed. But now the whole look of her changed. She put out a hand, caught his arm and held onto it. "It was just that you sounded so much like the rest of them. Killing's all they know — it's their answer to everything." She shivered, her voice falling into a whisper. "He won't ever forget the way you put your hands on him."

"Angel?" Matt said. "I didn't aim for him to." His glance crossed the creek. "We better get over there."

Her fingers tightened. "Wait —" she looked back. "Let them handle this — Angel's men. They've got rifles."

"Thought you were fed up with killing."

He felt a stiffness go through her and, following her gaze, saw a rider move out of those trees beyond the water. Just a boy by the look, in flare-bottomed trousers with a sash at his waist and a steeple-topped hat, chocolate gray in this moonglow, almost hiding his face.

Matt heard the others come up and watched the rider move down to the far edge of the water. The horse lowered its head, and while it drank the fellow watched them. Then he wheeled it away and rode off without speaking.

"Mexican?" Matt said.

Tara's eyes rummaged his face. Whatever she discovered must have reassured her. She put her horse across the ford and kneed it into the north, the rest of them following, the crew riding close-bunched — almost, Matt thought, as though expecting a bullet to tear out of the brush.

When they spread out again Tara's head turned. "By the way you spoke, you don't have any more use for Mexicans than I have."

"I had kin at the Alamo. Who was that?" he asked.

"One of the Flores tribe."

The ranch, when they reached it, had a lot of lights showing. Swinging out of a draw they came onto a flat and there it was, big and solid, without tree or shrub, laid out like a fort on the hard-packed adobe. All the buildings were squat, close-hugging the earth, constructed of mud and topped with low parapets slotted for rifles.

He noticed the heat trapped down here by the hills, took a look at the house with the twenty-post gallery hooked onto its front. But mostly he looked at the dark blotch of figures stiffly grouped round a lantern. Tara stared that way too and swerved her horse, the rest following.

Men, glancing round as she swung down, opened up to let her through. Tretisson, back of her, saw the pistol straightaway and presently found the lifeless hand. The man was sprawled face down and had one leg twisted under him.

They were all watching Tara. Perhaps she felt Tretisson's glance. She pulled her shoulders together. "Well! What happened to him?"

Angel, lowering the lantern, gave it to one of the others. "Pistol went off while he was peerin' down into it." The look on his mouth was like the smile of a cat.

5

Matt Tretisson ate at five o'clock in the morning with the headquarters crew in the big combination cook shack and mess hall. The empty chair at the head of the table was carefully ignored, but the weight of its implications hung over the meal in a kind of sour gloom. Both the gun fighter and himself drew a lot of covert scrutiny. Food was passed when Matt asked for it, but not one of them trusted him or showed comfort in his presence. One by one as their plates were wiped clean, the bunch got up and tramped out until he was left at the table alone.

He didn't care about that. His edginess came from the coiled prowl of Angel's stare which, while never quite meeting Matt's own lifted glance, had never strayed far all the time he'd been in there.

The shirt had almost certainly belonged to the dead man, and the empty chair at the end of the table was indication enough of the fellow's identity. He'd been the range boss, Scurlock. There'd be little done here until somebody else was picked to fill his place.

Matt threw a leg over the bench and got up, complimenting the cook on the caliber of his breakfast. The man glared suspiciously and went off muttering with his arms full of dishes. Matt stepped over to the door. The crew was loafing outside. The sun was bright above the rock slants. Talk fell away when the men discovered him standing there, and Angel, glancing around, met his stare with a look bland as sheep dip.

Matt reckoned he ought to get away from this place — ought to get, in fact, clean out of the country; but knowing this and doing it could turn out to prove considerable different if that girl had got her mind set. He supposed he could find out by asking for a horse but was fretfully reluctant to bring the issue into the open. Last evening he'd been lucky, catching Angel by surprise, but he found no ground for imagining he would be so fortunate again.

Tara Dow came onto the gallery, the brisk tap of her heels pulling a few heads around, but mostly the crew continued their sullen appraisal of Matt. The girl was coming across the yard, and he wondered again how much in his delirium she had managed to get out of him, additionally wondering if she'd passed it on to Angel.

He could understand cupidity — the insidious way greed fed on ambition and ambition on greed until nothing remained but corruption. Treachery, as Howisgrenn had proved, was no more than a natural by-product. What Matt could not convince himself of was that a woman could become so coldbloodedly practical as his suspicions — if true — must reveal Tara Dow.

He told himself it was absurd to imagine she could deliberately have brought about Scurlock's death. Capricious, self-centered, she might very well be — even strongly inclined to dramatize the most preposterous situation and relationship (that could come of the lonely life she led here); but to think. . . . *No!*

She'd been pulling his leg. It was the only reasonable answer. No matter what she had said he could never believe she could be so conniving, so wickedly heartless.

Just the same, Scurlock was dead. You couldn't get around that. Nor the gun fighter's fury. She must have known what Angel would do when he saw the shirt on a convalescing stranger at an isolated cabin. It was as inescapable as the interpretation the man had put upon it. She had deliberately connived to rid Bellfour of its range boss.

Eyeing her narrowly as she came across the yard, he realized how little he actually knew of Tara Dow. Up to this point the why of it had not greatly bothered him, but now his mind, leaping ahead, was fired by the sudden conviction that Scurlock's removal might not be the end of this.

He jammed hands in his pockets, thoroughly confused, angered and irritable. She looked so lovely he wanted to laugh at himself for the ridiculous fancies he'd been carried away with. In this bright morning light there was no place for such foolishness.

She came up quietly smiling and stopped a few feet away, her glance lingering on Angel before she fetched it around to include Matt and the rest of them. Matt, embarrassed, brought his hands out, rubbing the palms of them against the sides of his trousers. Angel was looking mightily pleased with himself, the bold curve of his mouth showing a proprietary interest as he followed her glance around the circle of faces. "We been waitin'," he said, "for you to name the new range boss."

Again her green stare shuttled over them, coming back curiously glinting to the regard of the gun fighter. "A hard choice," she said, making a little face at him. "Each of you, one way or another, has helped make Bell-four the kind of place it has become. I'm sure every one of you will continue to put the brand —"

"They know what you've done for 'em," Angel grumbled impatiently. "They'll not get outa line. By Gawd," he said, eyes skewering about, "if they do they're goin' to have me to settle with!"

Tara smiled. "Thank you, Angel. It's good

to know I can count on you." She took a deep breath. "The new man, Calico, will be my choice."

The gun fighter's face turned darkly blotchy. "By Gawd —" he cried in a choking anger, and swelled up like a carbuncle. He surged forward, hands fisting. *Do you know what you're doin'?"*

"Certainly," she said. "With this trouble coming up the job needs a cool hand, the kind of a man who can think under fire — not a hothead. On top of everything else I have got to be fair. How could I pick one of you over another?"

Matt stared at her stupidly. This was what he had been afraid she might do. "You could pick me," Angel said — "they wouldn't kick about that!"

Matt said, "I don't want the job," and the gun fighter's face twisted around, incredulous. But Tara said, "You'd never have gotten away from that posse except they were scared to come onto Bellfour."

Matt flexed his muscles. "I'll take your word for it."

He'd been right all along. Something she'd seen, or had thought to see in him, had convinced this girl that Matt Tretisson was the answer. He did not like any part of this deal. He had enough to keep watch on with that reward hanging over him, a bounty Howisgrenn's bank must have increased substantially.

He said out of the intolerable tightness inside him, "You've got a better man — any number of them, Tara."

"I'll have you," she said clearly.

"By God, I won't take it!"

Her eyes considered him unreadably. "You'll work for me or never leave these hills."

It was out in the open now, no more pretending.

Matt's anger was like a slow acid working through him, the scald of it creeping like a sparked fuse toward powder. Refusing the job had gained him nothing with Angel. The man's ugly look promised more would be heard from this.

Matt said with a desperate patience, "If you've got trouble shaping here, you'll want a man your crew can work with — you've got to have their confidence. No stranger could give you that. But —" he said, hedging because he had to, "I'm willing enough to work. I can help. I can give you another gun if that's what you're looking for."

He reckoned it didn't fool anyone. He saw the scorn and contempt on her face, knowing she knew he meant not even a word of it. She turned. "Take over, Angel. He's offered to work — you see that he does." She went off toward the house without another look.

6

She thought he was afraid.

But it wasn't just Angel. If only he'd had sense enough to leave that goddamn bank alone!

He became suddenly aware of an ominous silence.

The dart of his glance blurred over stone faces, shocked to a stop by the thrust-forward jaw and blazing eyes of the gun fighter. "By Gawd when I speak you better make out to hear me."

Was the man ready now? Had he taken his precautions or was this spleen from the grudge carried over from last night? Matt read hate in that look and felt the ragged edge of tensions which might snap at the blink of an eye.

"Sorry," he said, "I —"

"Get a pick and a shovel." Angel waved a hand. "This here's Juke. You'll take your orders from him." He wheeled away to lay

66

out the work for the rest of them.

Juke, Matt saw, was a knobbly-nosed man with his face squeezed around a mammoth cud of cut plug. He wasn't much bigger than a small snort of beer and looked old enough to have come over on the Ark.

Matt followed him to what looked to be a tool house and took up the shovel and pick he pointed out. The old man swabbed at his face with a sleeve and unloaded a jawful of molasses-colored spit. "Goin' to git power-ful hot. Mebbe you better unshackle that shell belt."

Matt didn't want to do it. He didn't want to encourage any misunderstandings either. He passed over the belt with its holstered Colt and picked up the tools. Juke motioned him ahead. "Off back of them yuccas an' bear to the left."

They crossed a lush field and another grown to cockleburrs and white-flowered thistles with cocoa-colored patches of bare earth showing through. "Rainfall's been spotty — most generally is till you git up past the mountain. Ain't a frog in that country's ever learned how t' swim."

"That what the trouble's about?"

"Mostly it's sheep. Swing north a bit here."

They came to a low ridge and Matt saw

the graves. There were five, all unkempt and all mounded with rocks. "To keep off the coyotes," Juke observed, mopping his face again. "That big un's her ol' man — six foot three an' God, what a wallop. I seen him knock one feller clean through a barn door!" He let go with some more tobacco juice that near half blinded a dozing ring-tailed lizard. "No better off now than Scurlock."

"He get shot?"

"Rattler got 'im — there's a heap of 'em around." He bent a sly look at Matt and scuffed about for a while, finally beckoning. "Reckon this'll be about as likely a spot as any."

"What are we fixing to do?"

"You're diggin' a hole. Quit gassin' an' fly at it."

Matt eyed the stony ground, dry and hard almost as a baked steer horn. He let go of the shovel. He blew on his hands and swung the pick. It went in about an inch. Matt looked the ridge over. "We better plant him somewhere else."

"You'll plant him right there where I said for you to or you'll ache a heap worse afore you git done with it."

Matt discovered Juke scowling across the barrel of a pistol.

He rolled up his sleeves and went at it again. The sun burned like a branding iron. There wasn't a breath of air stirring. After about twenty minutes Matt straightened up for a breather. "Six long by three deep," Juke said from his place in the shade of a yucca. "Like to see a man take pride in his job."

Matt scowled at his hands. "This the best pick you've got?" The wood was so dry the iron kept sliding down the handle. One of these times that heavy flange was going to catch him.

Juke grinned and spat. "You ast for work. You're gettin' it. Ain't nothin' wrong with that pick a little elbow grease won't cure."

Matt took up the shovel and got the loose stuff out. Be lucky, he figured, to be done in time for supper. He went back to the pick. Next time he stopped Juke said, "Where-at did you know 'im?"

Matt looked around blankly.

"Scurlock," Juke said. "His shirt you got on, ain't it?"

Tretisson pushed back his hat to dash the sweat off his forehead. Wasn't much he could say without telling the whole truth. He shrugged, picked up the shovel and felt it torn from his hands.

Black powder smoke swirled above the

69

barrel of Juke's pistol. "One thing you better learn fast around here is to answer when you're spoke to."

"Was the snake that killed Dow a two-legged one?"

The old man's eyes showed a leap of light, but it wasn't anything a man would want to cotton up to. "About Scurlock," he said around the bulge of his chew — "you aimin' to tell me or do I got to dig it outa you?"

The gun went off again, and Matt stared bleakly at his own belt draped across Juke's shoulder. "I never saw the guy before in my life."

Juke chewed like an old goat and presently motioned Matt back to his work.

By noon there were seven broken blisters on his hands, and his spine felt as though he had popped half his vertebrae. There were spots before his eyes, and the inside of his skull throbbed like a cut leg. He staggered out of the hole and Juke, getting up, said, "I'll go fetch us some water."

Matt stumbled over and fell down beside the yucca. There was no shade now, but he was too whipped to notice.

It was night before they roused him. He spent the next day in bed.

He got up stiff the following morning and trailed the rest of them over to the cook shack. When he came out they were roping their horses. Juke came over and passed him his shell belt which Matt took and buckled on, brushing a hand across the gun in its holster. Juke considered its hang and shook his head. "Too high for you to be any good with it." He clapped a hand on his own, and the barrel leered at Matt from the slashed-off end of that 'halfbreed' holster. "Where'd you be if I was minded to let go at you?"

Angel's face came around. "When you're done playin' John Wesley Hardin, that feller's wanted over to the house."

With the hand still fondling the butt of his pistol Juke winked at Matt brazenly. "Must be in high favor. I notice she ain't never ast you over."

Angel, looking balked and mean, swung into his saddle and rode after the crew.

"Plumb cultus," Juke grinned.

She pulled open the door before Matt could touch it. "Come in," she said, "I'd better look at that hole again."

He followed her down a dim hall to a kitchen that was done in curly maple and cheerful with sunlight flooding in through chintz curtains. The sill of each window and two-thirds of the table was lost in the greenery of potted plants. Beside the short-

71

handled pump in the sink were more plants, bright with blossoms. Tara pulled out a chair. "Don't stand there. Get that shirt off."

A kettle stood simmering on the back of the stove. On the uncluttered end of the table Matt saw shears, a roll of gauze and a wizzled-up leaf pinched from one of the plants. It reminded him of Scurlock and put hard glints in his stare. He got out of the shirt and straddled the chair, but now that he was ready she seemed almost to have forgotten him. She stood by the stove with a pan in her hands, obviously turning something over.

She was dressed in blue gingham with a tight-fitting bodice, and Tretisson, watching, could feel the pull of her, the promise, and wondered how he could think of her with anything but loathing. He fought a conscious attempt to deceive himself.

"I'm not going to," he said. "Might as well forget it."

The green eyes tipped around, still indrawn, only half seeing him. "Not going to what?"

"Rake any chestnuts out of the fire for you."

The lights changed in her eyes. The red lips smiled.

"You're a witch," he growled, unaccountably angered.

Her eyes laughed back at him. She had no need of words. Her expression — the whole look of her, brought him out of the chair, uneasy and restless. It was odd how a smile could turn a man's knees weak.

Despising himself he went toward her, seeing her eyes change, growing larger and darker until all the room was caught up and dissolved in them.

He took hold of her, pulling her forward, knowing she was willing. Her lips were cool, suddenly fierce, demanding.

Horse sound hammered through the walls of this moment. Booted feet struck dirt, came pounding over the planks of the gallery flooring. She would have ignored it, but Matt stepped back, glad to find an excuse. Her eyes, bright as daggers, scarcely veiled her irritation. "It can't —"

"You'd better go."

He listened to the strike of her heels in the hall, the rasp and skreak of the opening door. A man's excited tones filled the quiet. Tretisson caught the word "sheep" distinctly. Tara's voice lifted, calling Juke, ordering him after the departed crew. When she returned her face was composed, but the hard edge of something was thinly back of her stare.

She was excited and angry and yet inordinately pleased, so on fire with her notions she didn't care what he saw. She was like a purring cat in the sinuous sleekness of her serpentine grace, as collectedly cool, as arrogantly confident.

The provocative curve of her lips showed the tip of her tongue, mocking the bleak look of him. "Well — aren't you curious?"

He marveled she could appear so completely freed of her frustration. She was like a chameleon in the swiftness of her changes. He considered a moment. "Should I be?"

"Anything that happens around here should concern you. Anything which threatens Bellfour must threaten you."

"Maybe," he said dryly, "I've got past the trembling stage."

"No one ever gets past being afraid for himself. Your destiny is here. You can't get away from it."

"What a man can't get away from he will finally have to face."

"You see that? Scurlock never could. He thought because he had worked for old Flores. . . . He was a fool!" she said, dismissing him.

Tretisson stirred uncomfortably. Pinning her down was like trying to nail sunlight. Could it all be in his head — in his imagination? Much of it could; he was forced to concede that. But Scurlock was dead and Matt still had the shirt.

He said, "About those sheep —" and was stopped by the look of her.

"Yes. Those sheep." She was taut, gone still again. "I'm going to keep this ranch . . . every league, every acre."

Tara Dow at the linecamp was one thing. Here at headquarters she was something else, the driven part of her more forcefully in evidence. Perhaps he only noticed it more. When he offered no reply she said, "Don't make the mistake he did."

This made no sense at all to Matt though she was still, evidently, on the subject of Scurlock who had loaned her the shirt Matt had just taken off. That had been a mistake which had cost the man his life, but it was not likely to have been the one she was referring to.

"Whatever it was he rode up here to tell you, that fellow sure managed to get under your hide."

She went over to the stove and filled the pan with water. "When a girl comes into a place like this, she's considered fit prey for every brand in the country. If I'd listened to Scurlock they'd have stripped me. He said the way to get along with people was to try to understand them." She said, eyes flashing, "I understand them all right. They thought I'd be a pushover."

Matt sat down in the chair. She put the pan on the table and picked up the shears. "When my stock disappeared they found their own losses greater. It took a while to convince them. They shot at my riders; we shot some of theirs. We folded three spreads up before they decided to call the dogs off."

She'd got most of the bandage cut away from him now. Still covering the wound was a piece about the size of a silver dollar that had clotted into the scab. "I don't think," she said, "we'd better monkey with that." She passed gauze around his chest two or three times and tightly tied it.

He picked up Scurlock's shirt. She went to the sink and washed her hands. "The biggest problem I've had since Dad died has been right here on my doorstep — the Miranda Grant. Roughly forty sections in the shape of a wedge, the point of it driving like a lance at Bellfour's heart." The way she spoke you'd have thought it was her own heart. "You crossed it," she told him, "coming over here."

She had a hip against the table. But now she pulled away, obviously striving to get herself in hand. "The Grant is held by a

Mexican with a batch of handles long enough to lead a horse to water. Born on the place. There all his life, lazing out an existence for himself and a rabble of half-Yaqui in-laws by selling off chunks of it whenever they begin to run short of frijoles."

She crinkled her eyes at him but he saw her contempt, sensed a tension behind it he could not account for.

"They made a habit of butchering Bellfour beef until we kicked horses out from under a few of them. They took to stealing it then. We ran a bunch of their cows over a cliff and Flores — that's his main tag — screamed like a stuck pig. He even went to the law." She smiled a little grimly. "No sheriff would come out here."

He found that understandable enough. It made a pattern any small rancher with big neighbors would recognize. But the girl was too tense. Her eyes never left him. He got the notion she was listening to her words as she used them, and he wondered how much of what she told came out of fact.

She said suddenly, harshly, "Now we get to the guts of it. To avoid further friction we took the Point off his hands. Bought it and paid for it — and now he's put sheep on it. *Sheep!*" she exclaimed as though no crime could come up to this.

Tretisson got up and stuffed the shirt into his pants. "That was one of their crowd we saw the other night?"

"Do you think anyone else would have the gall to be seen there?" She waved him toward the door. "Tonight," she said, "they're going to think the sky fell on them."

7

A sickle moon hung like a suspended scimitar low down against the western blue, draping the valley in a spider-web haze as Bell-four, seventeen strong, came up out of the draw with Winchesters naked across their laps. Fantastic buttes crouched in stony contemplation. There was no jingle of bit chains, no rowel noise to warn of their passage; only the protesting creak of stretched leather got through the quiet rhythm of hoof-falls.

Staff-lifted bell-shaped flowers of the yucca came out of the gloom like the ghost-pale nimbus of fog-shrouded lamps and fell as silently behind. There was no talk. Each knew the score, each knew his part and when to play it.

Tara rode in the van, Angel to the right of

her, the sleeve of Matt's borrowed jacket occasionally brushing her left elbow. He didn't know what thoughts held those others, what hopes, what dark fears lurked behind their dim faces. He was determined to get out of this country as soon as might be. He had no intention of going back to Bellfour.

Tara Dow with her figure and that mop of red hair was too much on his mind. He had enough to fear — discovery by Howisgrenn and the Quitaque Pool, backed by the law, or reunion with the robber band. The fruits of his banditry were things he'd have to face, but until he'd decided which road he would travel he wanted no further involvements.

This chaparral breed she had gathered about her were about as unprincipled and vicious a coterie of cutthroats as you'd be like to come up with if you scraped the whole border. A man could as soon put his trust in a confederation of coyotes!

What in the world kind of woman would trail with such a pack? Was she mad or was ambition — lust for power — the thing which drove her? Matt knew only that he wanted no part of this. It wasn't his fight; he didn't mean to be pushed into it. He needed to keep this in mind. He couldn't do it around Tara.

What he really wanted was to get as far from Texas as a good stout horse could take him. If Gurd Pace and his saddlemates had not yet discovered him it wasn't for lack of trying. They would look a long while to get their hands on that plunder. And if this crew of Tara's ever got wind. . . .

Matt pulled his lip down.

Flores was a fool to invite trouble with Bellfour, knowing the kind of outfit it was. A fool or a man desperately bent on reprisal! A fool either way, Matt told himself bitterly. But he couldn't help feeling an edgy twist of compassion for anyone who'd got this pack of gun rowdies after him.

He hunched impatient shoulders, tugging up his collar against the increasing chill of these high altitudes. Twisting the reins about the brass knob of the horn, he pushed both hands in his pockets to get the numbness out of them. The girl had planned this well. Nothing but chance could ever save Flores' sheep, and she had cut chance down to where it looked like a sliver. The man — if he was doing as Tara claimed — would have guards posted and plenty of help, but he would hardly be expecting trouble from the direction of his own headquarters.

Matt saw the three men who had been

picked to mislead Flores' attention drop out of the file and disappear into the east. They even moved like coyotes, he thought, staring after them.

A lonely night, one peculiarly made for the stealth of such an enterprise. A decimation raid — a man might as well see the truth for what it was. She had told them to kill sheep, but she must know as well as Matt did that once guns got to blazing all targets would look alike to them. He didn't care for Mexicans himself, but lives were lives. After all, those poor devils were people!

He had damned well better be watching himself. As a stranger to this bunch he stood suspect until proved.

The creek was getting close again. Through an overlay of branches he caught the glint of the moon on water as Tara altered their course to fetch them deeper into the dark tree masses. The way pitched more steeply. They reached a crest, and the trail shelved downward in sharp slants as they neared the stream's bed. "Careful, now," she cautioned. "Keep your eyes out for these rocks."

She put her horse into it, the gun fighter kneeing his dun in behind her. The water lapped against its belly. Matt pulled his own feet out of the stirrups. He saw the rocks then. The dark gleam of their heads coming out of white froth made his stomach crawl. It would be almighty easy to make a racket in this place. . . . He pushed the urge away from him.

After the others were across Angel swung into the lead, another pair coming up and wheeling into the dark flutter of branches. These would be the muscle men, picked to take care of Flores' lookouts. The rest of the bunch would be concerned with the sheep, which were to be run into the rocks.

They hadn't given Matt a rifle. He still had the belt gun Juke had returned and took his hands out of his pockets as Tara's horse came about, her eyes hunting him. According to the plan the remainder of the crew were due now to spread out, and this was what he'd been waiting for, the chance to get off by himself for a moment.

Four riders filed past, disappearing to the left of her, climbing into the brush that fringed this escarpment. "Watch the noise," she cautioned. "Camp's just below here."

The willow leaves trembled, softly whispering in the dark. Matt let four more of the crew slip by, grimly waiting, before he wheeled his horse up into the line. Tara's hand reached out, catching the cheek strap, stopping him.

It caught him off balance, for there was still a man behind him and his swiveling glance discovered it was Juke. Tara said, "You'll stay with us."

The muscles knotted across Matt's stomach. He'd had his chance to warn Flores and passed it up, too afraid of the risk. Now, unless he could rouse the man's camp, he was caught up in this with no way to get out of it. The risk was redoubled, but he slapped hand at leather, fingers curling around gun butt, and triggered three times. This brought nothing but dull clicks, and Juke, back of him, chuckled.

The sound of it goaded Matt into a fury. He struck Tara's horse and, flinging around, struck at Juke. Juke saw it coming. He threw himself to one side but not enough to escape it, the downsweeping barrel smashing into his shoulder. He tried wildly to right himself, failed and was gone. *"Cuidado, Flores,"* Matt yelled, *"look out!"* and felt his mount stagger as the girl's horse slammed into it.

Matt ducked the whistling quirt she swung at him and savagely kicked her horse in the kidney. The animal bowed, shrilly squealing. Tara cursed. Her mouth was open, still swearing, when Juke's gun went off.

The light betrayed him. Matt, flattening,

drove into the dark fringe of brush. All through the night guns were lifting their racket. With Juke back there someplace Matt had to keep going. The ground dropped sharply. A pile of brush leaped into flame a hundred yards ahead of him, another pile kindling off to the right. This forced him north toward the creek again. Matt raced for its banks. Someone yelled almost under him. Two rifles hammered flat explosions from the willows and one bullet, ripping across the skirt of his saddle, made him jerk up his leg and veer into the sheep camp.

The whole flat was in uproar, men dashing about crazily, guns crisscrossing the shadows with powder flame. Bleating sheep were everywhere underfoot, rushing this way and that without sense in their terror. The shoulder of Matt's horse struck a man, sent him reeling, and off to the left of him someone cried out. A wave of horsebackers tore through the camp, shouting, shooting. The sheep wagon went over with a splintering crash, and out of the dust of this muzzle lights winked. Three saddles were emptied and one horse ran off dragging something behind it.

Matt's own mount screamed. He flung clear as it folded, and a great shout went up as he plowed into a thicket of golden-balled huisache. A frozen sickness gripped the pit of his belly as black shapes closed in, firelight glinting off the lift of their weapons. His knees went shaky when he saw it wasn't himself they were watching but a wall of riders plunging through the bleating sheep. A burst of lead raked the open. Arms thrown out, one of Flores' men suddenly spun, crumpling into a whimpering heap. Another staggered; the rest, in a panic, dove frantically for cover.

Matt, lifting his pistol, let the hand drop, an Indian grimness settling into his look as one of the riders broke away from the sheep. Thirty feet from Matt's thicket a boy-slim figure in a big Chihuahua hat had come out of the firestained shadows, looking to be in a daze, peering about as though unable to understand what was happening. He must have discovered the horsebacker. He went stone still, abruptly whirling, crowding everything into a crazy run.

This was the fellow they had seen at the creek the night Matt had gone to Bellfour from the linecamp. Both hands showed empty and he ran like a woman.

The man on the dun — the one who'd quit his companions — had a rope in his hands. Now he shook out a loop and came spurring to cut the kid off from the wagon. The noose flew out. The runner stumbled, pitching sideways, jerked down hard as the horse stopped short. Matt, suddenly afraid for him, knowing the boy was roped, broke into the open, bringing his gun up.

The roper put his horse about not ten feet away — so close Matt saw the flash of his spurs, only then remembering his gun wouldn't fire. He flung himself at the horse, trying to catch the bridle — missing. He made a grab for the rope as someone back of him fired. He saw the horse stagger. The rider, twisting around, kicked out at Matt viciously. Matt caught the leg and spilled the man from the saddle.

He struck the dirt on his back, one flying boot taking Matt in the kneecap. Matt fell across him, paralyzed with pain. He took a hard right just over the belt. The fellow got both hands around his throat. Matt felt as though his eyes would pop. He struck the fellow in the face with his gun barrel. The hands fell away. They came onto their feet breathing hard, weaving, wild-eyed, Matt bitterly knowing he couldn't take much more.

It was then that he realized who this was, that it was Angel. The man moved in, trying to finish Matt. A loose stone turned under

Angel's shifting weight and the blow fell short, swinging the Bellfour man half around. Before he could recover Matt hit him again across the face with his six-shooter. Angel yelled, stumbling backward, reeling into the capsized wagon. He caught hold of it, groggy, eyes stupid with shock.

Somebody yelped in Matt's ear, "Kill the son of a bitch!" Matt was vaguely aware of knowing that voice, and realized then there were men all around him, that the horse had been stopped. He saw the rope on the ground. The voice cried again: "Beat his brains out! Bust him silly!" Somebody shoved him, sending him stumbling off-balance into Angel. Arms like steel bands closed about him, wrenching a gasp from him; his gun hand was trapped within the constriction of this grip and he could feel his ribs bending.

He heard Angel grunt and felt himself being lifted. Somewhere in his head an alarm began beating. Angel was moving now, turning, and Matt could sense the man's feet probing the ground underneath them. He tried every way he knew to break away from those crushing arms. Angel dug his head deeper into the cage of Matt's ribs, inexorably squeezing while continuing to wheel. Matt kicked at his shins, attempted to knee him, but the man was like a bear in his stamina and single-mindedness. Nothing Matt tried seemed to have any effect at all on him.

No longer being able to see it he knew the wrecked wagon would be squarely behind him. He caught one of the gun fighter's ears, savagely twisting. The man broke into a staggering run. It was no time for squeamishness, the fellow meant to break Matt's back against that wagon.

He felt the stickiness of blood as the flap of ear tore away from the man's skull. Angel roared like a gutted bull. Matt fell sprawling as the arms let go of him, rolling over and over to get out of the man's way. He caught one blurred glimpse of Angel grabbing at his guns. Then something exploded against his head and he went down a skittering spiral that seemed to hammer every bone in his body.

8

The voices at first seemed as far away as something recalled from forgotten years, as formless and hazy, too vague to identify. He tried to slip back into that soft and warm place from which they had roused him, but they went on and on, continuing to nag from the dim edge of consciousness. Finally, exasperated, Matt pushed up and looked around.

He was in a house he didn't recognize, in a room spartanly furnished. A picture of the Christ looked down from a wall, and lamplight, coming through a partly opened door, disclosed a chest of drawers and one hidebottomed chair. He was on a bed, huge, four-posted. He twisted to look down at himself and discovered with some surprise that though he still had his pants, the borrowed brush jacket and Scurlock's shirt were gone.

He thought about that and swung bare feet to the floor, feeling the coolness of packed earth, strangely liking it. Then his head started pounding with all the violence of a rock crusher. When he could think again he remembered the fight and gingerly lifted an exploring hand. His hair was clotted with dried blood, and there was a knot on the back of his skull like a hen's egg.

His ribs were sore but he could not find any breaks and the wound hadn't opened. The uncertainty of his whereabouts bothered him almost as much as the pain in his head. He stared at the wavery gypsumed walls and the voices grew louder; one, pitched higher, sounding bitterly angry.

One thing presently got through to him. All the words he was able to sort out were Spanish, so he was not at Bellfour.

He got off the bed and, when his head eased a little, looked around for his shirt. It didn't appear to be in the room, but his holstered gun and shell belt were hanging from the back of the chair. He buckled the belt around him and reloaded the pistol from the half-filled loops. It didn't seem likely Juke would have tampered with every cartridge. He stood a while, listening, trying to decide what he'd better do next.

If this was Flores' headquarters he would be no better off here than at Bellfour. But they'd be watching their horses after that business of the sheep. He moved over to the door, easing it open a bit farther, seeing the nearer part of an empty hall. The light, evidently, was coming from a room off the far end. The voices were clearer but were still only sounds. He couldn't catch enough words to make anything out of them.

Pouching the pistol Matt drew a bleak breath as he moved into the hall and eyed a line of closed doors. A hall was unusual in a house styled by Spanish Americans. In a country wild as this they generally preferred to build in the form of a square, with the rooms giving onto an enclosed open patio into which their horses and dependents could be hustled in the event of an attack. The light and the continuing haggle of voices came from behind a door which stood ajar.

Probably a council of war, Matt decided, debating once more the wisdom of showing himself. He might be a prisoner, but he hadn't been bound. He could still slip away or make a good job of trying. There was nothing wrong with his legs. Still, he did not think they would take him far if his host decided to prevent it. A bold front, he guessed, would be his best bet.

He went on down the hall and pushed open the door.

A pair of faces came around at opposite sides of the room, but it was the man directly in front of him that caught Matt's look and held it. He must have been in his middle seventies, a great oak of a man, broad of shoulder even now, very alert, with bright eyes staring out of a jowled face topped by hair as black as an Indian's.

He got out of the chair, showing his age a bit more in that fumble of movement, in the creak of old bones, but with the eyes very alive and looking wonderfully shrewd as he came to his feet with a courtly bow.

"Buenas noches, señor," he said in a voice that was like a dove calling. "Be pleased to make my poor house yours — have this chair," he invited, pushing forward his own. "You are very welcome —"

"Don't be sure about that," Matt said gruffly. "I rode in with Bellfour."

"No matter. This is your house for as long as you will use it, and all that I have is yours to command. Please make yourself comfortable," he said with simple dignity. "I am Felipe Eleazar Flores y Miranda. This place was given to my people one hundred and forty years ago and in all of that time. . . . But I forget!" he exclaimed, clapping a hand to his forehead. "Allow me to present my daughter, Carlotta."

With more than the suggestion of a twinkle he waved a hand across the room and Matt, twisting his head, recognized the girl by the clothes she still wore as the "boy" he had saved from Angel's rope.

He blushed for the look of the pants she had on her, for the way they were molded skintight to her legs — a man's pants with slashed bottoms in the Mexican manner, and the scarlet sash wrapped about a waist that wouldn't have filled his two hands. Really, the women in this country. . . . He remembered his manners, bobbed his head, said "Pleased to meetcha," and was turning away when the tight-jawed look of her pulled his glance back.

She said with her face stiff as parfleche, "Meeting some people is about like finding a snake in your bedroll."

Matt's mouth dropped open. The old man's eyes showed his shame. He said in a shaken voice: "Carlotta!" and Matt saw her chin come up. Her father said, "You owe your life to this gentleman's courage," and his face grew dark with the baffled mixture of his emotions. No penitence touched her glance. "It was a trick," she said, "to get him into your good graces!"

"Enough!" the old man shouted — "I will hear no more of this!"

The girl's eyes, Matt thought, were like pieces of flint. Her father shook his head. "She is not herself," he apologized. "It is the shock . . . the. . . . Who can tell what goes on inside the temple of a woman?" He spread his hands with a Latin eloquence, then turned around. "And this is my right arm," he said graciously, "my . . . how you say?" He looked at Matt appealingly, pushed a fist through his scraggle of whiskers, grinned and said brightly: "*Fore* man! Señor Gurd."

Across the length of that lamplit room Matt's eyes met the unwinking stare of Gurd Pace.

Pace was swart and bald-headed in a blue wool shirt grimed with dust and dried sweat. Matt was appalled to find him here.

"What do they call you, mate?" Pace said, and Matt could feel the cold mockery behind that slate stare.

He pulled himself together. "My friends call me Calico."

Pace said, grinning, "Well, that's good enough for me. I can tell by the cut of your jib we'll be friends." He cocked his head in that gesture Matt so well remembered, and his deep-throated laugh rolled across the room.

Matt was reminded how infectious that laugh of Gurd's could be when he saw the quick response it got from the old man. Don Felipe's broad face relaxed in a grin, and he nodded his head with a pleased approval. *"Seguro si,"* he said, beaming around, "we shall all be friends as the good Lord intended. Will you not have a cup of café and some tortillas and beans — at least some cakes of my daughter's making and a little sweet wine? The grapes were grown at Rosswell by an uncle of my wife —" he made the sign of the Cross, "who rests in God."

He offered up a silent prayer, then clapped his hands. Like a jinni popping out of a bottle a *mozo* appeared at the door.

"Here — hold on!" Matt growled, determined to ask for the loan of a horse. But when he saw the shape of the old man's face, the hurt in his eyes, he sucked back the words in a silent curse. He could leave, he supposed, just as well in the morning. He caught the girl's black eyes. "I'll take the frijoles," he said, "and the coffee."

Pace conceded he would take a snort of the wine. Carlotta shook the stiff mask of her face, and her father gave the servant the order. "And find a shirt for our guest. These nights," he explained as they turned back, "grow cold. Will you wash your hands, my friend?"

There was a silent rebuke in his bow to the girl. He led Tretisson into a small room off the hall, its dirt floor recently swept and dampened to keep down the dust. There was a couch, a chest of drawers for linen, a chair or two and, on the chest, an olla of water and a glazed earthenware basin. There were also a few coins of gold and silver. "Yours," his host told Matt, "if you happen to be short. All of my house is at your service."

"Much obliged," Matt said, and peered

around at him skeptically. "What are you fishing for?"

The man looked perplexed.

"How long you been doing like this?"

"All my life," Flores smiled, "and my father before me. It is the manner of our people."

Matt, repressing a shrug, washed himself and dried on the freshly laundered towel he was handed.

Ponderous inch-thick shutters reinforced with hand-wrought iron made the window secure and kept out the cold night air. The door was of oak, carefully joined and heavily hinged. The whole place had the solid ruggedness of a fort and had probably many times served as one. The patina of great age was in the dull gleam of its smoke-darkened timbers, and something about it took hold of a man.

Tretisson felt this. Even so short a time ago as yesterday, had anyone suggested a house of wood and dried mud could have character he would have laughed. Bellfour had left him cold but this. . . . He felt a grudging touch of envy as he looked at Flores and thought of the joy and heartaches, the laughter and tears, the passion and violence this old place must have known. You could almost hear the forgotten voices in the whispering shadows just beyond the edge of consciousness.

His host indicated a short jacket the *mozo* had left on the couch. "If there is anything else you would like and do not see —"

"I'd like a horse," Matt said bluntly. "I'll have to leave you in the morning."

Don Felipe, suddenly grave, set his lamp on the edge of the chest and considered Matt. "I had been hoping we might persuade you to stay." The servant was back on sandaled feet holding out to Matt a shield-fronted shirt of gray wool which he got into. He noticed the rancher, as the *mozo* helped him on with this, covertly eyeing the scabbed-over gunshot wound Tara had doctored.

When the servant left Flores moved toward the door. "The Good Shepherd in His infinite wisdom. . . ." He squared tired shoulders. "Well, no matter. We all have our crosses — even that arrogant witch at Bell-four. When you go, take the choice of my stables."

There was something about this old man, like his house, which one newly meeting him found it hard to ignore. It wasn't a thing to be exactly defined, more a kind of quiet comfort, of simple dignity and peace. Yet Matt could sense a deep unease in the man. *We all have our crosses.*

With a sidewise half-angry final glance at the coins stacked so neatly in the shine of the lamp Matt, grunting, followed his host down the hall.

In the *sala,* or living room, he took the chair Flores proffered and pulled it up to the heavy table where a place had been laid on bleached sack cloth. The pungent odor of chili drifted up from the plate which had been bounteously laden, and the smoking coffee, without cream, was the color of Carlotta's eyes.

Matt tried to think while he was eating (and Don Felipe rambled on of past experiences with Indians) what Gurd Pace would do in the morning when he set off on Flores' horse. There'd be trouble, that was certain. Whatever Pace believed, he'd want his cut out of the loot and he would want it pronto.

The hour was late — it must be crowding two — but no one appeared to be thinking about bed. Don Felipe, when Matt had finished, passed around some black cigars. Pace, who'd been dividing his interest more or less equally between Carlotta and Matt, took two, stowing one in his pocket. Matt shook his head. The old man put away the box. "A glass of the vino perhaps? For the stomach?"

Matt held up the wine and admired its color which reminded him of Tara's hair. "What are you doing about those sheep?"

An indragged breath emphasized the startled stillness. This was the sixty-four-dollar question — definitely a subject Matt should never have put tongue to, but he was fed to the gills with all this goddamn politeness, all this horsing around.

With a visible reluctance Pace pulled his stare from the girl. Her black eyes which had stayed distrustfully on Matt from the moment of his return sharpened into blazing anger. Even Don Felipe was not entirely immune. A hardness crept into the look around his mouth. "My people are out trying to save what they can." His cheeks became mottled with outrage. "Is there nothing this woman will not dare?" he cried bitterly.

Matt held no brief for Tara Dow, but he thought that was putting it a little bit strong, trying to push the whole blame for trouble on her. "You were asking for it when you put the sheep over there."

"*Caráí!*" the old man sighed. "Where else should I put them? First she steals all my cattle her *chaparralistas* do not kill —"

"But you *sold* her that land. You gave up all your rights to it."

"Gave up — what you mean?" burst out Flores, in his agitation forgetful of his precise and proper English. "She say she buy? She tell you that?"

"She said she'd bought the Point and paid for it to avoid any further friction."

"She lied!" Carlotta spat, unable longer to keep still. "She has never paid for anything!"

"That's right," Pace nodded. "She pulled one out of the hat on us there."

Don Felipe dragged a hand through his scraggle of whiskers. "She *said* she would buy it to avoid further trouble —"

"But it was a trick!" Carlotta cried. "She sent that wicked one, Angel, and he came with two men. He had a great sack of money which he put down on the table and a paper he had brought — a transfer, he said. But I can read the English! It was a quitclaim. My father said no matter so long as it stopped the killing."

Her breasts pushed against the cloth of her shirt with the anger that was in her. "When all was in order and my father had signed it, the two hombres with Angel, *as you very well know!* whipped out their *pistolas.* That *cochino* put the paper away. Then he picked up the money with a laugh and rode off!"

The seething eyes with which she raked Matt's face were like the fires of hell, he thought uncomfortably.

The story was not too surprising, wholly compatible with what he had observed of Angel's character. The fellow had acted on his own, seizing opportunity by the forelock, setting himself up with a tidy stake. He had no intention of running, Matt thought — not so long as he might grab Bellfour too.

"And what were you doing while this was going on?" Matt asked, swinging around to confront Gurd Pace.

"I wasn't here. It won't happen again."

"You were here when they ran off those sheep."

Pace froze into a long motionlessness while the devil behind the slate-colored eyes considered Matt shrewdly, finally showing a faint amusement. "You'd like to see me go foggin' over there, I reckon."

"It's what you're paid for, isn't it? To protect this outfit from things like that?"

A darkness roiled those eyes like smoke. Don Felipe, his glance swinging curiously from one to the other of them, interposed before his scowling range boss could speak. "Mine is the blame for letting them go. It is a business for the law —"

"What law," Pace snorted. "If you mean that law at the Siding, it won't lift a finger long as Bellfour's got that paper. Any sheriff shows up, it'll be to work against *you*." His dark face swiveled to Matt. "Tell him for Christ's sake to wake up, will you?"

Matt frowned. "What happened to Angel?"

"He let him go, too," Pace said disgustedly, and got out of his chair to tramp the room, savagely flexing his fingers. His black store pants, shiny, creased with wrinkles, were too long at the crotch, too short in the leg, barely covering his boot tops. They'd been in too many rivers, but they didn't make Pace look foolish. With those two guns at his hips, he looked exactly what he was — an exterminating son of a bitch.

Of course Bellfour had the law up its sleeve, but Pace was talking for himself. He didn't want any law brought into this. He didn't give a hoot about his job with Flores. His whole purpose was to fix things so they could hide out here a spell. Matt looked at him carefully. The man didn't care a snap of the fingers what happened to Flores or anybody else. What he had on his mind was that hundred thousand and a place to hole up till the heat blew away.

Pace turned back to the rancher. "You had the right idea when you hired me, mister, and if you aim to save what's left of this spread you better throw off the hobbles and give that crowd back some of their own."

The old man shook his head. "Two wrongs do not make a right," he said tiredly.

"You can't put out a fire by shuttin' your eyes!" Pace shot back. "You light another fire to fight it or you get burnt out!"

Flores looked at Matt. "What do you say, my friend?"

"Not my fight."

"But if it were?" the rancher prompted.

Wanting only to get out of there Matt shook his head.

Flores sighed. "I knew they would come when I put the sheep out, but I was angry. All their lives my people have fought for this place and I had no thought . . . but these are not *Indios.* They are not cowboys. Our poor weapons are useless — like everything here. We are an antiquated lot. When we see the wolves we are too much like the sheep. We do not reason, we run."

"I can hire you a few that won't run," Pace said. "Let that woman get away with this, and she'll snatch the fillin's right out of your teeth!"

Once more the rancher's eyes flashed in

Matt's direction, but Matt ignored their mute appeal, remaining doggedly silent. Flores, turning back to Pace, said, "Bellfour is strong, her men well equipped, well mounted. Even her reputation is against us. All who have defied them in the past are gone. Where then will you find anyone?"

"I'll find 'em," Pace grated, and suddenly flung himself backward as the lamp exploded in a clatter of glass. Burning oil lifted blue heads of flame. The darkness was filled with the strident fury of rifles. The wild yells of raiders lifted over the yard.

9

Matt could see the girl fighting to put out the burning oil as he sprang past her father to get under the nearest window. Pace was already firing, the frantic rip of a scream attesting the deadliness of his skill.

No one had to tell Matt it was Bellfour out there — this was the answer to that set-to with Angel. Or maybe Tara Dow was behind it. She'd been wild enough the last he had seen of her.

He came onto his knees fetching up the barrel of his pistol just as a volley of shots took most of the glass from the window.

"Whole damn outfit!" Pace snarled through the uproar, viciously jerking fresh loads from his belts. Another volley shook the side of the house. Again someone yelled as he drove lead into the murk.

Something dropped off a wall behind Matt. He got his piece of a look. The yard was black, crisscrossed with the leap and flash of powder streaks. Bellfour had come off their horses and the implication of this thinned Matt's mouth, suggesting as it did a fight to the finish.

It was not a happy thought for a man who had figured to be well away in the morning. He saw two muzzles spit from a corner of the building diagonally across, and a Sharps beside him loosed its deafening roar. Over there something fell, became a motionless blotch. Matt glanced at Flores with a new respect.

He tried then to visualize the placement of this room, knowing it was in the front part of the house with the hall door back of and somewhere to the left of him. Both windows faced the yard, and the outside door — giving onto a veranda — was beyond and to the right of Pace who held the farther window. The table was behind Pace, barely discernible now that Carlotta had smothered the flames from the oil. Matt put a hand on Flores' shoulder. "Who else is in this house?"

"Tomasito only, and his wife who does the cooking."

"Find them," Matt said, "and tell them to watch the back of the place. Better give them something to shoot with."

He turned back to the yard, giving the fight his full attention. The shapes of three dark buildings showed clearly. He saw the partial lines of two others to the left. Directly across from where he watched was what he judged to be a bunkhouse or communal dwelling for the unmarried help, apparently untenanted; but vague movements beyond effective range of his pistol indicated this likelihood had not been lost on Bellfour. They'd be hard to budge, but he hadn't any lead to waste on long chances.

A bullet ricocheted from the beehive fireplace and another struck the unlatched front door low down, kicking it partially open. Carlotta wrenched past and slammed it shut; he heard the drop of the bar and told her to get away from it. She stayed where she was, probably more to defy him than for any better reason. He heard Pace growl something about cartridges. "Perhaps a handful of forty-fours, *no más,*" she answered; and Matt said, "Get them."

He lost track of her then. "Watch it!" Pace snarled and Matt, peering into the lesser black of the yard, discovered something afoot between what he took to be a black-smith shop and the stables. "They've got some of the help penned in that last build-ing," Pace said. "They been tryin' to fire it. That's a hay wagon they're pushin'."

Don Felipe came back with his buffalo gun and Matt nudged him, pointing. The rancher hoisted the Sharps and went care-fully still. When it spoke a man dropped and the rest ran for cover. But some of Bellfour had got into the bunkhouse and rosettes of yellow and purple began to dimple its dark side. Slugs from this thumped and whistled about the windows, forcing Matt and the other two down, filling the air with dust and danger. They heard firing now from other parts of the house and Pace wickedly wished with a foul wealth of blasphemy for the Henry repeater he had left with his saddle in the stables.

Matt said to Flores, "I'm off for a look out back," and crawled the floor on hands and knees, keeping below the windows till he got into the hall. Behind him in the dark he could hear bullets thwunking into the boards of the veranda; one struck a roof support like a rock plunging into water.

Don Felipe, staring after him, considered how recklessly foolish he must seem to be — giving the run of the place and his trust to a man about whom he knew so aggravatingly little. Right now, out of their sight, he could be firing the house or slipping the enemy in, the sooner to overwhelm them. What did anyone actually know of him? Only the fact of the rope and the rough-and-tumble with the man who would have dragged Carlotta over the rocks. Suppose she were right and that ugliness was naught but a piece of play-acting, pantomime designed to put the fellow in their good graces?

But to what purpose? Surely, by their return, Bellfour intended to finish this now. The man was tough — anyone could see that, but not like Gurd, not like that scum who rode for Bellfour. There was a difference.

Flores nodded. It was this difference he was counting on. Whatever the man's connection with that witch it was finished, cut off when he'd pulled Angel out of the saddle.

Matt, in the hall, hurried on to the end of

it, flinging open a door behind which he'd heard voices. A dim shape was crouched with a gun by a window and another swept out of the close-by dark and became the girl in boy's clothing, Carlotta. *A princess they'd have called her in the old days.* "Here —" she said, and his hand was filled with the cold greasy feel of heavy cartridges. "For your pistol."

She brushed past, going on down the hall, swallowed by a mealy gloom that was almost blood brother to the blackness of his prospects. He stood confused, pulses quickening, restless and dissatisfied, needing to hit something and not knowing what. It was as though he plowed through a bowl of thick stew or were struggling in sorghum up to his armpits. Nothing made very much sense anymore but the need to get out of here and bury his backtrail.

Carlotta, too, was at odds with herself, despising her own vacillation and quickened breath, yet caught up, in spite of all reason, by inexplicable feelings of torment and excitement. The man was nothing but another tough gringo (of which this country had more than its share!) whirled up out of the dust of some faraway fracas, another gun-throwing drifter plying his trade for the highest bidder — and who could guarantee more than the witch of Bellfour!

She almost wept in her bitterness, in the blaze of her resentment. Nothing was the same; all the joys and quiet simplicity she had known were gone from living, all the customs of her people had been corrupted or discarded utterly since the coming of these *Yanqui* outlanders. There was no tranquillity anywhere. Of traditions they made a mockery, of the women they made whores. Who but a fool would trust them? Who but her father would take them in, cultivating the seeds of his own destruction!

Matt went over to the window as the shape fired again. He asked in Spanish: "How many?"

The *mozo* said, "Two, maybe three."

"Do you think they are trying to get in here?"

The man rolled his eyes. Matt could see their whites as the fellow's face came around. "Señor, who knows? The ways of these goats do not explain themselves."

Matt slipped back to the hall. The man's wife would be in this other back room; but, as Don Felipe had said, you couldn't count on these people in this kind of business. He remembered telling Tara not to count on her crew, but they would stick all right until

110

the going became considerably rougher than he had any hope of making it. Even though, temporarily, they were forced to fight in the open, Bellfour had all the advantage. They had mobility, the weight of numbers and the additional resource of being equipped with army rifles.

There was nobody in the next room Matt tried. He reckoned it wouldn't take Bellfour long to discover this. Give them another half hour and they would be inside. The house was too big, too spread out, for so few guns to hold it.

And there would be no quarter. Any man who surrendered would be lynched for a cowthief — they would want no witnesses to this night's work!

He ducked over and eased up the room's single window, crouching there, listening a moment to the guns. No need for him to wait. He had only to put a leg over the sill, and under cover of the night he could still get clear if he played his cards right and used a proper discretion. He didn't have to die here. He could elude Bellfour and Pace too with a bit of luck. It was what he'd been hoping to do, wasn't it?

But Matt knew, even as he toyed with the urge and found it practical, that he could not sneak away and leave Flores at Bellfour's mercy. The old man deserved better than this.

It was the kind of thing you might expect of Angel. Pace could do it and probably would unless he found some smoother way out of this jackpot. Not even the thought of that hundred thousand would ever stand in Pace's way if he were forced to decide between the loot and continued living. Trouble was — if Pace left — he would damn sure insist on Matt leaving with him!

Closing the window, looking grim as he nodded, Matt stepped back across the hall, more than half expecting to find the servant gone. At first glance it seemed the suspicion was justified. Not until he was nearly to the window did Matt, softly swearing, discover the man. He lay crumpled under it. Matt knew without touching him he would never get up.

Matt went back to the front room.

Pace, grimly silent, was still watching the yard, waiting for carelessness to put some-one in range. Carlotta was on the floor by her father who was reloading his single-shot buffalo gun. "We've got to get out of here," Matt said bluntly. "They've killed Toma-sito."

Carlotta, wheeling with a cry, disappeared into the hall. "Where would we go?" Don

112

Felipe asked; and Pace, suddenly cursing, growled: "They've fired that shack!"

Matt wriggled around to where he could look, hearing the derisive hooting of the Bellfour crew who now were waiting around like jackals for the trapped Mexican help to be forced into the open.

Out of the corner of his vision he saw the Sharps coming up. Pace saw it too and knocked the barrel aside before the old man could fire. In the flickering light Matt saw Flores' bewilderment. "Those are my people, Señor —"

"They're done for anyway," Pace said brutally. "The waste of one bullet ain't goin' to do them no good. We've got to get over to them stables."

Matt chewed on his lip and said, "I'll make a commotion at the front of the house while the rest of you slip out —"

"Oh, no." That was Pace. "We're all in this together and we're stayin' that way — savvy?" He stood with a loose-muscled slackness, but the guns were in his hands. "I'll be givin' the orders. His Nibs here, Don Felipe, would take it rightdown sad was you to get yourself rubbed out, mate."

Matt saw the grin on his lips, saw Flores watching.

Carlotta came in from the hall with her

cheeks the color of yeast in the fireglow, shepherding a short dumpy squab of a woman whose sobs leaked through her lifted hands and through the folds of the black shawl she'd flung over her head. The cook, Matt guessed — wife of the dead Tomasito.

He found it hard to remember he didn't like Mexicans in the quick rush of pity that thinned his lips. It was the *patrón,* Don Felipe, who took the bereaved woman into his arms. "There, there, *pobrecita* —"

"Hell," Pace said, "we got no time for tears." They could all hear the stepped-up racket of rifles. "They're shootin' 'em down like dogs out there. They'll be after us next." He pushed them into the hall. "Out! Out!" he growled, "pronto!"

Matt, in the little room's darkness, helped the girl through the window. The cook was more trouble in her voluminous skirts and Pace, swinging through after Flores, struck her. "Shut up!" he cried, ugly. "You keep on with that snivelin' I'll give you somethin' to yowl about!"

He slid along the house wall to the corner and peered around it. He growled, coming back, "This ain't goin' to be no picnic, but it sure won't get no better for waitin'. You first, Flores, then the girl. Calico can manage the cook and —"

"Don't you think perhaps —" Matt broke it off, seeing the wicked jump of Pace's pistols.

"I'll take care of the thinkin'. You just head for that tool house and keep this mewlin' female —"

"Look!" cried Don Felipe; and Matt, whirling, felt a trembling under him, saw a slither of men break out of the timber that concealed a slope at the back of the house. Angel's shout rocked at them and the shapes fanned out. Pace, covering Matt, shoved Flores' cook out into the open. Matt heard the bullets slap into her before he caught the sharp cough of the rifles. She fell with her arms clutched about her middle.

"Now —" Pace snarled, "get around the corner!" and cuffed at Matt with one of his guns. The mouth in Flores' shocked face dropped open, but Matt shouldered him roughly before he could speak.

There was only one corner they could go around — the one giving directly onto the front of the house, bright now with glare from the flaming roof. Matt was afraid of that brightness with the rest of Bellfour holed up across the yard, but this was no time to argue with a man who would just as soon shoot as shout.

He sprang into the lead, diving past Don

Felipe and the girl, reaching the corner first and throwing himself around it in a catlike crouch. There was a yell from behind and slugs kicked gouts of plaster from the wall as Carlotta and her father pressed panting on his heels.

Across the yard three of the Bellfour crew had come out of the bunkhouse and were caught flat-footed without cover by Matt's unexpected appearance. Matt flung himself sideways, laying his quick fire at them, scattering and stampeding them — dropping one of four others quartering forward from the stables. From the black offside of the tool house a man yelled, "Angel — Angel!" and suddenly stumbled, falling headlong beneath the galloping hoofs of a dark rush of horsemen tearing out of the heavy gloom back of the building.

"Down!" Matt cried at Flores and sent the girl, who was nearer, spinning toward the veranda. She caught a heel on the step and went sprawling as an Indian yell burst out of that pack.

All over the yard panicked Bellfour hands, trapped in the light of the flames they had kindled, were scrambling frantically to get under cover. Matt drove his last slug at a fading shape and saw the man reel but flounder on out of sight.

Matt swung away sharply, stumbling over a fallen man as he broke open his pistol to punch out the empties. A hand fastened onto him, saving his balance, and Pace blared furiously into his ear, "Get up on that —" but Matt jerked away from him, some compulsion sending narrowed eyes back and down, bringing an oath from his lips.

It was Flores there on the ground. The man's mouth was open and there was blood on his chin — blood in a great thickening stain on his chest. Matt heard the girl's frightened gasp; and she was there, bending with him, as he stooped and got both arms under the rancher. He wasn't sure for a moment he was going to get up with him, but he made it, the girl running ahead to throw open the door.

He heard a blast from Pace's guns, the hammers falling so fast it was a continuous roar; then he was past and onto the veranda, half hidden behind dark climbing vines from the search and slap of flying lead. He slid through the door, breathing heavily, sweating, lurching after the sound of the girl's heels. "In here —" she said, reaching out a hand for him. "Will you get off his clothes while I'm scaring up some water?"

He marveled that at a time like this she

could show such command of gringo idiom. She was a Mexican and running sheep in cow country but, beyond and above this, she was a woman and he liked the way. . . . *Better watch yourself, Tretisson. Don't let her grow on you. Breasts and bullets. . . .*

He pulled away from this, swearing, and got the old man out of his bloody clothes. He shook his head over the wound which was black and ugly, reminding himself his only concern around here was a matter of survival — his own, not someone else's. But he still had not got the girl out of mind when she was back with the water and the torn-up scraps of a sheet.

He shook out the struck match that had been licking his fingers, snapped another alight along the edge of a thumbnail. He didn't look at Carlotta but heard her low cry when she discovered the black hole. He worked the chimney off a lamp and touched the flame to its wick, ratcheting it down. He left her then, stepping softly, returning to the front of the house. The fight was over, the fire put out, Bellfour — at least temporarily — routed.

10

Reloading his pistol Matt stepped into the

yard, morosely considering the dark huddle of horsemen pulled up by the strident voice of Gurd Pace.

The range boss, spying him, beckoned. When Matt joined him Pace said, "Time to bust Bellfour is right now 'fore they get set again — see if you can make these damn fools understand!"

Matt questioned the men in his own fluent Spanish while they stirred uncomfortably, a few shaking their heads. The majordomo, he told them — and at the word one of them, eyeing Pace contemptuously, spat — felt they should push after the raiders, harrying them, carrying the battle to them before the syndicate crew had time to get organized.

A short man with bushy eyebrows — the one who had spat — appeared to have the say. He had a *vaquero's* muscular roll of shoulder, broad chest and lean hips. He looked a part of his horse as he sat there unmoving on his poor man's saddle, a pad of sacking stuffed with hair.

Wind flapped at his clothes in the gray, strengthening light and he cuffed at a knee with the ends of his reins. Another day, Matt noticed dismally, was practically at hand, and he was no nearer getting away than before. "Listen," he said, "is this hombre your boss?"

The man's face crinkled up and he swallowed, breathing hard. "The *patrón* has said so," he answered grudgingly.

"Then do his command," Matt snapped back at him.

The man twirled his reins. He took a squint at the clouds and stared woodenly at Pace who stood watching and scowling, not catching the sense of this. Pace had used Spanish in the house a while back, but it seemed from his look that his comprehension might go no further than a handful of picked-up words.

The horsebacker said, "We do not trust this one — this gringo *chingao* of the two *pistolas*." He eyed Pace again out of the corners of his cheeks. "I think this one has a devil riding his buttocks."

"He is a Texican," Matt said, pleased at the grimness that came into their dark faces. Sounds broke through the early quiet, the rasp and clank of shovels scraping into stony ground. The short man yanked his head around. "The goddamned *Bellfouristas* —" The eyes in the bristly brown short-necked face flared down at Matt like unsheathed daggers. "Do you know how many of our people have been killed? Seven men, three

120

women and four little ones — not counting the thing of Tomasito's señora!"

In the thin sunless light Matt saw the jut of their cheekbones, the way the short one's boot-brown grip convulsed the leather of his reins. Their hate and their fears, the wild breath of their furies, were all about him, goading Matt toward another choice, another decision. The chance to bring about Pace's destruction lay clearly within his trembling reach, delivered there by the *vaquero's* reference to the fate of Flores' cook. Matt had only to breathe Pace's name, to tell of the outlaw's part in that, to send every man in this yard against him.

The thing of Tomasito's señora, the Mexican had said, yet Matt held his tongue. For what if by some incredible fluke the man should survive! Matt had been shown Pace's way with a woman. Sweat came out on the flats of his hands, but he fought temptation and bitterly whipped it.

The short Mexican stirred. "I am a poor man, Señor, with little that was learned from books, but I can read the ground. Josefina was pushed. Her blood cries out —"

"And the blood of those others," Matt flung back at him harshly — "your kin, your own loved ones! Does this make no sound?"

The *vaquero's* face went pale and stiff. "I

am no coward, but should the living die also? How can we know this is no trap he would lead us into? And what then of the girl if the *patrón* dies too?"

It was the argument Matt had used on himself.

He turned back to Pace. "No use," he said, turning loose of his breath; and the range boss, blackly eyeing them, swore. Pouching his pistols he tramped off toward the house.

Most of the mounted crew moved away. Some, anxious-eyed, rode toward the smoke, some gravitating toward the sound of the shovels, others leading their horses in the direction of the pens.

Matt said to the short one, "What are you called?"

"Lágrimas," the man answered, which in English means tears.

An apt name. Matt nodded. "And what of the sheep?"

"By an intervention of God we found the most of them safe. We were bringing them when we heard the *arma de fuego* — the shooting. But for that . . ." He spread his hands and, shrugging, scowled.

Matt produced tobacco and papers, holding them out. Lágrimas gravely put together a smoke. *"Mil gracias,"* he said, bending over

Matt's match.

A loyal man, and obviously no fool. Pawing through his thoughts Matt was trying to decide how best he might put what he had in mind when bootsteps alerted him, squeezing his breath down. Gurd Pace was close, too close for comfort, eyes bright and cold as a magpie's. Matt watched the swing of them shuttle back and forth.

There was something crouched and calculating in the way they finally settled on him. "You've shown plumb handy at givin' orders — suppose you catch hold of a few for a change." He tossed Matt a key. "This'll let you into the stable's gun room. I want this place put under close guard. Arm everyone who can work a trigger — split 'em up into shifts. You understand that?"

Matt nodded.

"Put some life in it. When you've got it took care of come over to my office."

Matt found no chance for further words with Lágrimas; Pace sent him off with orders about the sheep. He probably suspected what Matt had been up to and would take enough care to keep them apart. It was not going to be easy now for Matt to get clear; the very fact of his having posted the guards would incline Pace to have him

123

watched all the closer. No need of misconceptions on that score.

But there was one gleam of hope still left. Pace, if there was trouble, would cut him down without compunction — indeed, on the slightest pretext. He would probably take a very real pleasure in any misfortunes which came Matt's way, but he would not kill him or order him killed except in the gravest extremity. He was much too interested in learning the whereabouts of that disappeared hundred thousand. Not, Matt thought, that this was much to take heart from. Pace had let it drop once that he had lived with the Comanches. Some of their ways could make death mighty welcome.

The diggers were still at it when he came back from posting the first round of guards. Bellfour had not got off too lightly. They had lost four riders on a permanent basis and some who had got clear would be in no great rush to be strapping on their guns again. Three of Flores' riders too were laid up. Neither side had been put out of action, but Dow, Angel & Company were bound to do some careful figuring before setting off a new full-scale effort; and if Tara were back of it she would be doubly cautious. By her own tell, Bellfour had too many enemies for her to risk coming out of another go so poorly.

Matt wanted to feel in his own mind it was Angel they were up against, that Tara was an unwitting tool in this business. Everything about the play by which these Mexicans had lost the Point appeared to stem directly from the mind of the gun fighter. It was the kind of deal you would expect from him. He was out to get Bell-four for himself — Matt wouldn't see it any different; and the man's quickest means was obviously through the girl. He had only to make himself indispensable. By Scurlock's death he had come in one jump from hired man to range boss, and that pattern, once followed, must inevitably repeat itself. Only through the medium of further violence could he insure her need of him. Hence Flores. By cheating the Mexican outrageously Angel had set the stage for his endeavor.

If Flores had done nothing the man would have found some other means. No fellow who could make himself necessary to a woman would ever doubt his ability to eventually twist her in whatever direction he wanted.

Matt felt sorry for the girl — sorry, too, for the mess she had gotten herself into; but he was not her keeper. He had his own black problems and time was of the essence. He felt sorry for these Mexicans too, but he had overstayed his grace in this country and tonight someway he would have to get out of here.

All of Flores' best horses were kept in the stables under the care of three *mozos* who did nothing but look after them. Matt had already seen the one he wanted — had discovered the horse while he'd been arming the guards. A big black. A Spanish Barb they called El Tosco.

He was skirting the tool house, bound for the majordomo's quarters, when Carlotta stepped into his path. It may have been chance which put her here at this moment, but it was apparent she was not displeased. She stood squarely, solidly in front of him, compelling him to stop. He dragged off his hat. She said, eyes wide and searching, "I suppose you came from Texas too."

He didn't know by the *too* if she were comparing him to Pace or to the fly-by-nighters Tara Dow had gathered round her. She had a right to bitterness. He conceded this much, nodding. She had a dress on now and her hair in the Spanish manner, held in place by a high-backed comb. It improved the look of her considerably and narrowed his eyes with a sharper notice.

She was not a pretty girl, but she had resolute wholesome features and a way of carrying herself that caught a man's attention. She was younger than he'd thought, and the clean-limbed lines of her disturbed him, someway turning him more somber, more dissatisfied with his prospects. It was her eyes that bothered him most — black like her hair and filled with confusing lights that could blind a man if he looked too long. He glanced away edgily, staring over the yard with a spurious interest.

She said, calling him out of this barricade of silence, "How long have you been at Bell-four?"

"Week, more or less."

"Perhaps," she said tentatively, "I have misjudged you. How well do you know their riding boss Scurlock?"

"Never knew him at all. The man's dead. Angel's top screw over —"

"You're lying!" she cried, every line of her vibrant with shocked, angry protest. But the black eyes believed and it seemed she must surely fling herself at him, so wild for a moment was the whole outraged look of her.

"The shirt . . ." she whispered. "So that's why you were wearing it! You killed him —"

"No." Matt caught her wrists. "Listen —"

127

he said, and told her how he had come to the lineshack, of the shirt and all that had happened thereafter, omitting only the more personal elements — the traps Tara had baited with her looks and her words.

Gradually, as he talked, the last of the resistance went out of the girl and a kind of bleak hopelessness pulled down her shoulders, leaving him with the conviction that if he turned loose of her she would almost certainly fall. He surprised himself by wondering if he truly believed that or merely found it convenient as an excuse to keep hold of her.

She resolved his dilemma by releasing herself. Stepping back she said with sudden decision, "My father was right. There is nothing that witch would not try to get us out of here. She killed him as surely —"

"He was dead when we got there."

"No matter who pulled the trigger, it was she who cocked and pointed the gun." Her black eyes swept his face. "She wanted him dead — she was afraid of him I tell you! She knew. . . ."

"Knew what?"

"That she had lost her hold on him. You didn't know he was part Mexican? He was boss *vaquero* for my father once, but she hired him away from us — with her body, I

128

think, not her honeyed words. Rafael knew she was no good —"

"You are letting your anger run away with your judgment. It was Angel, not her, who pulled that trick with the money. Angel —"

"Two of a kind," she said with cold scorn. "And do not tell me about Rafael. Some way she discovered he was spoiling her plans. He came here, you know — only last week he came to warn us. She must have seen him or come onto his tracks; then when you came into the picture she made a new scheme — this thing of the shirt."

Matt considered her uncomfortably. She'd got it all mixed up, and she was mixing him up in his own mind. He didn't want to see Tara like that. It was Angel. . . .

"I think men can be very blind," she said, watching him. She was obviously deeply thinking about it. "You blame the man. Perhaps he did steal the money, but she is the one, I tell you. She was back of it.

"So! You scowl. You do not believe that. She is *muy habilidoso* — very skillful. With *men!*" He saw the scorn in her eyes. "From what you tell me, from all that has happened, I think she wished more to get rid of Angel than Rafael. For Rafael she could fashion an accident, a fall from his horse or a stone from the rimrock; but for Angel. . . .

No, she is afraid of that one. He is very jealous. She must have hoped you would kill him."

She turned as though to leave and then swung back as Matt asked gruffly about her father. "He breathes," she said, and put a hand against the wall.

"He won't make it," Matt said darkly. "You better get out of this," and saw her eyes flash.

"I do not ask your advice, gringo. You had better get out yourself, I think. It might be if you had not come. . . ." She glared at him, flushed and resentful. But the wildness passed, and she said with her lips curled, "Take a horse if you will, but do not stay here, because that witch —"

"You talk like a fool!" Matt said, fed up. "You saw what Pace is when he pushed Josefina."

"Pace? That was Gurd. . . ."

"Sure — Gurd Pace!"

She'd gone back half a step, eyes enormous. She said in a stifled voice, "The *bandido?*" reflex carrying a hand to her throat.

Matt said grimly, "I see you have heard of him." He noticed also how gray her cheeks had become. Before he had time to think what he was doing he'd told her his plans and said: "You'd better come with me."

"With you? *Me?*"

It was then that it hit him. He clamped his mouth shut, aghast.

But he needn't have worried. She almost laughed in her scorn. "Do not alarm yourself, gringo. I go nowhere. And if ever I did go, it would not be with you!"

11

The first things Matt noticed when he stepped inside the Grant office were the two glasses and the bottle on the desk beside Pace's feet. These, bare and grimed with the dust of weeks, took Matt back to the slash-and-run fight they had waged against Howisgrenn and the hired slug-slammers of the Quitaque Pool.

If there was one thing Pace detested it was cramming his feet into a pair of damned boots, and the reason this so riled him was because, out of vanity, he insisted on buying them two sizes too small. This had used to bring a chuckle from Tretisson. This morning he didn't bother even to scrape up a smile.

"Close the door," Pace said, grinning across the width of the room. He pulled off his hat to cool his bald head and wriggled his toes in the way Matt remembered. "I'm not what most folks would call a celebratin' man — as mebbe you've noticed. But a thing like this. . . ." He broke into a laugh. He cuffed his leg with the hat. Through the dust this struck up Matt saw the gun in his lap.

Pace had aimed for him to and had himself a real guffaw. Then, still with that Judas grin, he said, "We'd about give you up."

"I got shot."

"Bad, eh?"

"Bad enough to spend a week at Bellfour. On my back."

Pace clucked and sighed and put on his hat. "We mighta worked somethin' out. How come you didn't tie up with that outfit?"

"All you want to know," Matt said, "is what I've done with the dinero."

"Wouldn't mind hearin'," Pace allowed, eyes brightening — "not that I ever figured you'd run off with it."

"That's for sure. Well, it's safe enough. No need to worry."

Pace flashed his hard grin. "I leave all that for the other guy — remember?" But impatience chased the grin off his face, and he picked up the pistol, twirling it by its trigger guard. "Let's get to the great unfoldin'."

"The money's cached."

"That figures."

"A cache is no good without it's kept secret."

"I guess you know how I feel about secrets."

Matt's glance poked around above a wry little smile. "That gun ain't goin' to get it out of me, Gurd."

The bandit's face turned black and sharp. His feet slapped the floor, and one long stride fastened his fist in Matt's shirt.

Matt made no attempt to get loose. He said, staring into those ugly eyes, "I sort of reckoned you might have forgot who was boss —"

"No son of a bitch is goin' to double-cross me."

"No one's trying to. Yet."

Matt could see the clash of desires in that face, the intolerance, fury, balked viciousness and greed. There was also, sending its cracks through these things, a belated and baleful caution.

The hand finally dropped from Matt's twisted shirt. Cold remained a hard ball in Matt's belly. He managed to say in a voice that blessedly stayed in key, "All you're holding is a busted flush. You better think this over."

It wasn't bravado put his back to Pace then — or maybe it was. One thing Matt Tretisson could well believe. If Gurd Pace ever found that loot, Pace would kill him.

He spent most of that day catching up on lost sleep. At five Carlotta woke him. Worry and weariness had lengthened her face and her eyes looked dull, but she had courage — she had a lot of it. "I've left a plate of food and coffee —"

"How is your father?" Matt cut in, swinging legs to the floor and reaching for his boots.

She shook her head. She turned away. "He's asking for you. Come as soon as you've eaten."

He stamped into the boots and, going over to the bowl, drenched his face in the tepid water. He toweled dry and discovered the girl was still there, idle against the door-frame, watching. "All right," he said. "I'll be along."

She held her ground. "This *bandido* — how long have you known him?"

"Pace?" Matt said grimly: "Long enough not to put any trust in him." The tough planes of his cheeks showed a sudden ir-ritability. "What I told you still goes. If you want to pull out I'll do my best to get you clear. You must have friends —"

He stopped because of what he saw in her eyes. All the anger born of his frustrations surged up in him. "You can't handle that cross-grained bastard! Try using some sense before it's too late!"

"My home is here — you think I run away from it?"

Matt went over and took a long drag at the coffee. He picked up the plate and came back and sat down with it. He remembered the bottle and glasses on Pace's desk, and considered Carlotta while he stuffed the food into him. He didn't much go for this chili-soaked garbage — nor for Mexicans either, he reminded himself. She could give a man a fight, he thought, but all the odds were against her.

He tried to make her see that. "Gurd ain't alone in this country. He's got men around someplace."

"I have men around, too."

"Sure, and they've got to be fed. What are you using for money?"

She tipped back her head. "We have a little," she smiled. "In the bank at Mule-shoe."

Muleshoe. Howisgrenn's bank!

Matt swallowed hard. *I ought to tell her,* he thought. But how?

He finished his food in scowling silence. When he handed her the plate Carlotta said, "You will come now to my father?"

Matt's shoulders moved impatiently. He had a pretty good notion of why Don Felipe would be wanting another word with him. But this girl had her pride.

He got up off the bed. "I'll see him, but I'm leaving tonight. And if you've got any sense you'll get out of here too."

She glared back, eyes flashing. "For why do you care what I do?"

"I couldn't care less," he said, brutally. "But that Pace —"

"I think you know that *bandido* too well. I have seen how he watches you. When you go, I think, that one will go also."

He stared at her bitterly and picked up his hat. He strapped his gun belt about him and followed the clack of her heels down the hall. He wouldn't permit himself to think beyond his need to get away. Nothing else counted — by God he wouldn't let it.

Don Felipe lifted the sunken eyes in his gray face and tried to smile when he saw Tretisson. The old man hadn't long to be with them and knew it. He moved a waxlike hand about an inch across the covers, and the hovering girl bent over him.

Flores' voice was so feeble Matt, at the foot of the bed, couldn't make out the words, but Carlotta said, twisting her face around, "He wants the *capataz* — the foreman — to be here also."

Matt said, "You'd better hurry then."

Her eyes struck back at him, filled with hate. She whirled out of the room. Flores, watching, muttered *"Agua,"* huskily.

Although it was gone too quick for him to be sure, Matt had thought to have caught in the old man's glance a hint of half-humorous approval. He got the glass, propped the rancher up and held it so he could drink. He didn't take but a swallow. When Matt let him down Flores' eyes seemed much brighter. His voice had more body. "You are running from the law — *no es verdad?*"

The Texan shrugged.

Don Felipe said, as with a touch of regret, "What man has not some secret that he hides? In each one of us, I think, there are some things which do not show. In that table is a . . . a paper."

Matt, stepping across to it, pulled the drawer out a little and lifted a faded and yellowing parchment of tiny ribbons and much red wax. But Flores shook his head. *"Otro,"* he gasped, and Matt held up another not so large, and white, twice folded. The rancher's eyes said yes and Matt shut the drawer and came back to the bed and put the paper in his hands.

Pace came into the room with the girl, throwing a darkening scowl at Matt; and the rancher, noticeably weaker, said to his daughter, *"Pluma, tinta."*

She looked curiously at the folded paper and then, suspiciously, at Matt. She fetched the quill and ink without remark, and while Matt once more lifted the old man up she held the paper. Flores, grunting and wheezing, laboriously scratched his name and slumped back. *"Testigo . . . testimonio,"* he said in a barely distinguishable whisper.

She took the paper and quill to the table and bent over them. But suddenly she straightened, throwing down the pen. "No!" she cried, whirling, furious.

She appeared about to tear whatever it was in two when Pace, reaching across Matt, grabbed it out of her hands. He backed away with it, scanning it, his expression strangely wooden. Matt guessed it was written entirely in Spanish. "I expect," Matt said, "he's wanting you to put your name to it."

The old man's face confirmed this. His wrinkled lips shaped the word for witness.

Pace, scowling, peered from one to the other of them, finally picking up the quill and taking the paper over to him. "Where?" he said; and Flores, with great effort, put a shaking finger to the paper.

Carlotta, springing forward, cried, "You fool, he's trying to give it all away!"

Pace's brows drew down. "Give what away?"

"*La tierra* — the land! All the land he is possessed of!"

The bandit blinked at her. "To *me?*" He looked astounded. And then a startled comprehension swung his face to Matt. "Of course!" Now a grin crossed his teeth. "What's wrong with that? His land, ain't it?"

"He's out of his mind!" Carlotta cried, looking very nearly to be out of her own. "This — this foreign devil. . . ." She stopped to fling herself again at Pace, trying to tear the paper out of his hand. The bandit easily warded her off and, bending over the table, signed his name with a flourish.

Looking around then to see who he was to give it to, his eyes went shrewdly narrow, and he stuffed it into the right hip pocket of his pants.

12

Carlotta's eyes bulged glassily.

She was staring at her father, the back of one hand squeezed against her teeth. Matt knew without turning that Don Felipe was dead.

He braced himself, trying to think and then trying not to while the cold shivers chased up and down his back. If the old man had given this land to him, it was because he didn't know what he was doing.

Matt said, looking hard at Pace, "I'd like to see that paper."

Carlotta curled her lips with a contempt that openly denied this profession of ignorance, but the bandit, caring nothing for the how comes of Flores' beneficence, declared with a bland assurance, "When you're ready to talk turkey mebbe we can fix up a trade."

He had no need to put it plainer — that paper for the bank loot. The man cared nothing for personal property.

Matt felt a tightening of his throat as though a rope were settling round it. Sweat cracked through his skin as his mind plunged against the invisible toils in which Flores had trapped him. His face twisted with anger. But the old man had done his work too well, binding the Texan as with links of steel.

Matt had one bitter thought of going to the law, of giving himself up just so they grabbed Pace with him; but it was not good enough. It left Carlotta faced with Angel, with Tara Dow and her gun-hung range roughers.

He cursed aloud.

Pace, watching him, grinned. "For a feller that's just come into a ranch you show a mighty daunsy look, mate. Give it back to her if you don't want it."

He strode off with a laugh to give some further advice to the second shift of pickets getting ready across the yard to relieve the guard Matt had posted.

Matt felt hollowed out and useless.

Flores had nailed him with the gift of this land, imposing an obligation he believed Matt incapable of repudiating. The old man had saddled him with defending Carlotta's future by giving him her inheritance, understanding Matt better than Matt had understood himself.

The girl, of course, had been right about Pace. When Matt left, Pace would follow him. To the ends of their lives if he had to. And Bellfour . . .

Matt, snarling, shot a look at the girl and

turned with his teeth locked to go after Pace. But she caught him, breast heaving, and spun him around.

Grief and shock had changed her face, but nothing, it seemed, had altered her convictions. She had no conception of the coup her father had managed; she saw only in Matt another of the hated strangers who'd swarmed into this country on the heels of Kearny's conquest, flesh and blood reality of the ruthless greed, corruption and ruin visited upon her people at the hands of this alien horde.

Twilight had crept into the room, but he could see the naked hate in her eyes and, on impulse, moved toward her, reaching a hand out. She sprang back, putting the width of the table between them.

"Lies!" she flared when he tried to explain. "You think I know nothing? Stay back — keep away from me!"

He caught the flash of bare leg and saw a knife in her hand, long and wickedly slim, its baleful glitter lancing into the shadows. He had had no intention of touching her, but a raging craziness suddenly got loose in him and he upended the table, flinging it savagely away from them. She struck out with the knife and he twisted her wrist. The blade, still dry, hit the floor with a clatter.

She whirled to run, but the wall was too near, and in these close quarters she ducked under his arm and jabbed with spread fingers. He saved his eyes but felt her nails rake his cheek before he knocked them away and grabbed her roughly against him.

"You damn wildcat —" he gasped, and furiously struck her as he felt the pistol wrenched away from his hip. He heard her sob, pant for breath as she staggered. He slammed her uncaringly into the wall, knocked the gun from her grip and, panting himself now, tried to get hold of her pummeling fists. She had a wiry strength, was surprisingly agile. Before he could pin them Pace said from the doorway, *"She wasn't included in that deed for the ranch."*

Matt fell back, suddenly shamed, seeing the scowls of those others crowding in behind Pace. They had seen Matt's hands on her, and this was all the bandit needed. He growled with a fine look of spurious outrage, "Take him, hombres!"

The *vaqueros* fanned out, deploying to envelop Matt, eyes bright with the remembrance to too many gringo villainies.

Anger climbed into Matt's throat like bile, but he stood stiffly unmoving, recognizing the futility of resistance. A fight was what

Pace wanted. Matt couldn't get clear, but if he roughed up these fellows it could strengthen Pace's hand, establish his right to cripple Matt with a pistol.

Years of hard work showed in those boot-leather faces. Insecurity, fear of future and all the mixed emotions of a vanquished people could combine — with Pace's cunning — to reveal their distrusted foreman in the trappings of a champion, a righter of wrongs which had been too long ignored.

Sensing Pace's game, Matt grinned at him toughly, saw the outlaw's cheeks darken. "Outside with him," Pace snarled, plainly aiming to salvage whatever he could from this. "Get off his shirt and spread him over a wagon wheel. We'll show this woman-pawin' *Tejano* —"

Carlotta said, "Be still, hombres! Listen to what I tell you! Put these gringos on the road to town — at once, without horse."

The men, confused, looked bewilderedly at Pace. "The *patrón* —"

"The *patrón* is dead. I have this place now," the girl said sharply. "Do as I tell you."

"By God —" Pace blustered, and stopped with his jaw dropped, eyeing Matt's pistol in the girl's lifted hand. How and when she had recovered it Matt himself had no idea, but it was plain she would have no qualms about using it. The skin tightened across Pace's cheekbones, and he froze into his tracks with a stifled breathing.

Looking slimmer and taller in the fading light the girl motioned Matt brusquely over beside him. "Tie their hands, Chico," she commanded one of the younger men; and this fellow advanced warily, bringing a piggin string out of his pants. "Ramón, have your knife ready. If either of them try to give trouble, use it. The bald head first, Chico."

Pace, who had been scowling, made an effort to straighten his face out. "Look — what the hell, I don't know what you're frothin' at but —"

"Tie him, Chico."

Pace said in a fury, "You want me to break your goddamn neck?"

The man backed off, but three others caught Pace from behind and jerked his arms back. With them holding him Chico tied him and then came over to Matt. Matt put his hands out.

"Behind him, Chico," Carlotta said.

In a way Matt had to admire her. She had been too upset to understand her father's strategy; or perhaps, understanding, had considered it too risky. She had no faith at all in Matt and made this plain by ignoring him as soon as the *vaquero* was done with his rope work. She thought the way to protect herself was to get rid of them, and she was going about it with no waste of time.

She glanced at the men holding Pace and, not trusting these precautions or even the ropes, bade them throw him. With one Mexican sitting on top of his head and two others wrestling his threshing legs, the girl bent over Pace and went through his pockets. She stood up when she got the paper and handed Matt's pistol to one of the men. Pace quit struggling and started cursing.

She waved a hand at the door. "Outside."

The fellow who'd been perched on Pace's head got up and the other pair, each of them hugging a leg, dragged him out of the room and bumped him over the splintery boards of the veranda. The *vaqueros* laughed.

Matt said when he could make himself heard, "You've still got Bellfour to reckon with."

The gloom was too deep for him to see her expression even when she came over to where they held him. "I have still got the ranch." There was a deal of satisfaction in the tone of her voice. She made a little ceremony of tearing up Flores' quitclaim, reducing the paper to tiny pieces which she threw in his face with understandable contempt.

Matt considered her dismally. "What have you done about the guards I put out? Have they come in? Have you sent the relief out?"

"Worry about yourself, gringo." She eyed him angrily, then waved him away. The two men who had hold of him started him doorwards. "Be thankful," she called, "I do not have you shot. I know who you are, what you've done."

Matt, stiffening, remembered the bottle and glasses he had seen on the desk by Pace's feet in the office. But he had no time to grasp why Pace had told her. The pair who had hold of him hustled him out.

Lantern light flared in the stables as they came into the yard. Some of the men standing around were guards posted that morning.

As they were shoving Matt toward the stables other figures blackly showed against the bobbling light. They were bringing readied horses off the runway into the yard. One, flinging up its head, shrilly nickered.

The fellow who had hold of this horse jerked the lead shank and, laughingly joking with one of his companions, got his face in the light. It was Pepe Morales, one of the half Yaqui cowboys Matt had put into the second string of guards Pace had been going to send out more than an hour ago.

Matt was disgusted. In typical Mexican hit-or-miss fashion the watch had been abandoned now that Pace had been stripped of authority.

13

Pushed into the light slanting out of the stables, Matt stared at Pace across the width of the runway. In the grip of two burly barefooted peons, Pace was quiet now, but the festering rage was as plain in his face as the blood dripping out of the gash where someone had struck him. Why had he told Carlotta about the bank? To let her know she had nothing but Gurd Pace to fall back on? To make sure she would not in desperation turn to Matt — to improve his own position by fostering the hope he might repay what she had lost?

Whatever the reason he would get no good from it now. She had no use for Matt anyway, though she might have felt different if Pace had kept his mouth shut.

A squatty Mexican came out of the blackness with the loose coils of rope, and with a flick of the wrist dropped its noose around Pace's neck. The bandit spat at him, swearing, but the Mexican, jerking slack from the line, went on and climbed into a saddle. The nervous horse nickered again, a lot louder, and four other *vaqueros,* jingling long-rowelled spurs, quickly mounted. One held horse was left — the high-strung gray gelding — still dancing about at the end of its hackamore, pawing and blowing and laying its ears back.

Chico, with Matt's belted pistol, came up with a grass rope. Suddenly the riderless gray twisted its head to look off toward the house. Three of the riders slanched around to stare likewise, one of these, muttering uneasily, crossed himself.

Chico reached out with his loop, but Matt flung himself backward, not quite breaking free of the pair who had hold of him. Carlotta strode out of the shadows as the *vaquero* struck Matt across the face with his rope. The nervous gray broke away, and at the same moment Angel's voice, wickedly lifted, sailed out of the trees masking the slope beyond the house.

One of the pair watching Matt lurched and stumbled. One of the horses, screaming crazily, went down. A steeple-hatted *vaquero* flung out both arms and went off his mount backwards as pounding hoofs beat through the racket of rifles and Bellfour's crew swept around the house at a gallop.

Matt, half blinded with the scald of tears churned up by that rope's end, used his head like a bull to send reeling the man still holding him. The white face of the girl swam into his vision and he cried, "Get me loose!" and saw her look at him without comprehension. Another Mexican pitched off his horse horribly gurgling and the rest disappeared like straws in a wind.

Matt bunted Carlotta at the stables' open doorhole as Pace, still trailing the rope from his neck, sprang across the runway, disappearing inside. Bullets struck baked adobe, and a horse tore out of the blackness, reins flying, coming within inches of running Matt down. "Juke — Juke!" Angel bellowed; and gunfire thunderously burst from the stables. Someone killed the lantern, Bellfour's charge broke apart and Matt in midstride was abruptly knocked flat.

He tried to get up and his legs were sponge rubber. Quick hands grasped and pulled at him. Someway he knew it was Carlotta beside him. Something tugged at his wrists and they were stiffly free. He got his feet under him, coughing, half strangled from the dust. He could hear the deep sob of the girl's labored breathing. "Please —" she gasped, "one more step," and a wall scraped his elbow and the reek of black powder made his eyes swim again.

He discovered they were inside the stables. He could see the vague shapes of crouching men, the bright lancing of powderstreaks as guns kept hammering their slugs through the din. He put up a hand that came away sticky slithery. Pace yelled for someone to "Hurry up with them horses!" and cloth ripped very near.

Carlotta said urgently, "Bend over." The touch of cool fingers brushed the back of his neck and something came tightly around his head like a hat brim. "That will keep back the bleeding." She pushed a gun into his hands — a Henry repeater, Matt guessed, by the feel of it. "Your friend," she said. "He kept it here with his saddle."

Matt was still pretty rocky. Much too mixed up and shaky to track down the elusive reason Carlotta had found for this surprising show of burying the hatchet. He turned from the hips to stare at her and brought his mind rather bitterly to consider what was happening.

He hadn't any real doubt. The Grant very obviously was fighting for survival. Bellfour had a reputation to live up to — a reputation, built on toughness, of always coming out on top. Last night they hadn't done it and, whether or not Tara had recognized this, Angel — nursing his own ambitions — would have been quick to see the facts. Any outfit riding roughshod over its neighbors was bound to have problems.

Bellfour might own the law in these parts but this, like every other facet of their position, was dependent on their continuing to be able to pipe the tune. They could not afford to be bested. They couldn't back up — the whole country would take this for weakness. The slightest evidence of that, and Bellfour with all its arrogance would be nothing but a memory.

And there was another side to the picture. They were in top spot because of the kind of men they had on their payroll. Tara Dow had known that; she'd done her best with Matt. Let those gun rowdies get the idea Bellfour was slipping, and they would run like the coyotes the great bulk of them were. If that crew ran out on her, Bellfour was finished.

All these thoughts passing through Matt's mind took no more than a second. In the next he was moving, running back toward the stalls and a turmoil of frightened horses, determined — whatever it might be — to spike Pace's intention. Pace had scared up some plan to help Carlotta out of this jackpot, something that depended on horses — he was yelling for them again; and the last thing Matt wanted was for the bandit to regain any influence.

"No!" Matt growled, waving back the first man he saw leading a horse.

"Por dondé?"

"Otro," Matt snapped — "out the back!" and ran past while the peon was still trying to turn the fractious animal around. There was danger in this, and Matt recognized it, for the matter of time allowed no margin for errors. At any moment Bellfour, having smothered all outside resistance, might set fire to the buildings or, in a charge, breach the stables' defenses. But he doggedly stuck to his purpose. "Out the back —" He told them all the same thing, shouting it at them as he ran past. He had to shout through the uproar to make himself heard — two he had to catch hold of and turn bodily. One of these, more stubborn, demanded suspiciously to know by what right he gave orders.

Matt stopped in his tracks. "Burro," he said, "where is your gun?" The sharp tone of his voice, the wild look of him, put the man in the wrong. A peon was nothing. A gun had real value. As the man stood confused before the enormity of his position, Matt pressed into his hand the key Pace had given him. *"Compadrito,"* he said, clapping the man on the shoulder, "I myself will manage this horse while you go to the gun room and make sure all are armed. Be diligent now. Pronto!"

He sent the man off with a shove of his hand, finding with astonishment the horse he had hold of was the black Barb, El Tosco, he had planned to get away on. In the Spanish, *tosco* meant tough. The black looked it. He had a long and lean underline, powerful quarters. And he had the kind of eye Matt liked in a horse.

The crash and bang of somebody's gun choked off on an empty, and through the ragged quiet Matt heard Pace's enraged bellow. The bandit, Matt guessed, had discovered what was happening with the countermanded horses. Matt realized he ought to get out now and that, with all this excitement, he had the chance and means of doing so. Pace, thrusting fresh loads into the pistol he had someway got hold of, was in a fine lather and apt — if he sighted Matt — to do almost anything.

Matt pushed through a back door still gripping El Tosco's reins and carrying the rifle Carlotta had put into his hands. The night was like ink out there, made blacker by the gloom from a grove of oaks. But this cover wouldn't long avail them.

Even as this thought whirled through his head flames burst from the roof of the distant tool house, plunging weird lanes of light through the foliage, revealing the horses and the men gathering round him. He saw the fright in their faces and the desperation too, and the snorting quivering animals acting up at the ends of whatever they were held by. Pace's swearing voice was coming through the stables, and off somewhere in the night Angel's bull yells were exhorting his gun crew to "Pour it into 'em! Pour it into 'em!"

Somebody raced through the darkness off to the right of Matt, between the stables and what was left of the peon's quarters. Searching slugs struck and screamed off the nearby hardpan, went *thwutt* against tree trunks and doorframe. Dust from the wall was sucked up by the wind from the blazing roof, and Matt piled into the saddle. Less than six feet away a Mexican grabbed at his stomach and jackknifed onto his face. At Matt's yell the others scrambled onto their horses and went streaming after him around the far side of the stables.

Pounding into the yard Matt saw a running man in high-heeled boots suddenly whirl in mid career and, diving, scramble back of a horse trough made of oozing two-inch plank. Two others of the Bellfour crew, also afoot and apparently part of a new attempt to rush the now almost undefended stables, flung around and high-tailed it for the flickering corner of the building nearest the flaming tool house. The antiquated rifles of the Mexicans dropped both of them.

The fellow back of the horse trough had his gun going now. Three jets of water simultaneously spurted from the side which protected him. He jumped up, visibly panicked, and Matt knocked him sprawling with a slug from the Henry.

The mounted bulk of the Bellfour crew burst suddenly into the north end of the yard, yelling and firing like a bunch of Comanches. The *vaquero* nearest Matt coughed once and dropped limply. Another man reeled and half fell from his saddle. Matt was lifting his voice to order them into the dark of the woods back of the house when four other horsemen, racing between buildings, came up on Bellfour's flank, gouts of powderflash stabbing into the swirling dust. "Chihuahua!" these cried above the crash of their weapons. The yell put new heart into Matt's men and turned them. Bellfour, caught thus as in the web of a net, tried to cut back, but fire from the stables blocked them off in that direction. Panicked, they broke like splatter, every man for himself, spurring madly for the hills, Angel's blasphemous shouts wholly wasted.

It was not Lágrimas who had turned the tide this time but what was left of the group under Chico who had been going to move Matt and Pace off the ranch. Recklessly now Matt's three riders, flushed with easy victory, rushed to join their pursuit of the stampeded raiders. "Come back, you fools!" Matt yelled, but they ignored him, racing blindly after the mirage of glory.

Matt pulled up.

The tool house roof had fallen in. The night still glowed above it, but the light coming through its burned-out door and windows did not reach him and only meagerly revealed the deserted yard with its motionless huddles of dead men and horses. He counted five of the latter. He was too sick to count men.

He looked a long time toward the silent stables and reluctantly guessed he'd better hunt for Carlotta. Pace must be around someplace too if he hadn't been killed, which Matt figured was too much to hope for. Fishing some of the cartridges the girl had given him out of his pockets he reloaded the rifle, grimly keeping his eyes peeled. He would have to watch himself after this around Gurd. He really ought to clear out while the chance was available. He aimed to, but first he had to find the girl.

Swinging down, still gripping the rifle, he led the black horse toward the horse trough. A little risky, he supposed, to be showing himself so openly; but he wanted to get his hands on a pistol. He kept out of the light as much as he could.

He had to cross the ruby glow of two windows or go a long way around to come up to the trough, but the Bellfour man seemed likelier than any Mexican to be packing a .44, which was what Matt was after, since cartridges for it would also fit the Henry, and he had only two extras after reloading. He didn't want to quit the Grant as short as this on fire power.

Just the same it made the hair on his neck crawl to show himself against the red of those windows. If Pace happened to be looking . . . He would have tried one of the other Bellfour targeted riders except that the only others he knew about were the pair who'd been dropped by the corner of the stables. Although Matt had never particularly thought of himself as being at all ingrown about anything, he was a lot too bashful to step knowingly out and give Pace the chance of putting a gun on him.

14

He got up to the trough without anything happening, but the fellow he had shot was no longer lying there. Peering around, Matt increasingly felt the pressure of time. If that hardcase had been able to drag himself out of sight he could likely work the trigger of that pistol Matt had come hunting — and probably had it. Unless it was buried in the muck from the punctured trough.

Suddenly sweating, Matt stepped back against the horse. His scrinched-up eyes raked the roundabout shadows and looked again at the pair of sprawled shapes by the still-too-bright side of the stables. He wasn't about to go over there, gun or no gun.

His glance, coasting on, caught no suggestion of motion but his mind rebelled against staying here longer, and he was reaching for the horn of El Tosco's scuffed saddle when he discovered Carlotta at one side of the stable's main entrance.

She appeared to be watching him, but she

was too still about it, too unnaturally quiet — almost, Matt thought, as though a gun were held on her; and his mind leaped to Pace, every instinct urging flight. He found himself crouching like an animal at bay and straightened, guiltily outraged. "You all right?" he called, and she stared at him, wordless.

Matt turned El Tosco toward him, swinging gingerly into the saddle — more to make sure he kept hold of the black than for any more definite reason. He had a dread right now of being left afoot. He had never seen a man who could match Pace with a gun, and the way things were going there was no saying what the fellow might do. Gurd was a primitive. Wholly capable, if sufficiently provoked, of completely forgetting that hidden hundred thousand.

Clinging to the shadows Matt stepped the horse nearer the girl, suddenly reluctant to speak at all but knowing he had to. "All your help that was mounted took out after —"

"I know." She said without moving, "Gurd thinks I've seen the last of them."

Matt held the same opinion. Angel, twice driven off, would be wild enough to seize any chance to even the score. And there'd be plenty of places to ambush men as foolhardy in victory as that bunch from the

Grant. "Where *is* Gurd?" Matt said.

"I don't know."

"Are you sure," Matt said, "he ain't standing there back of you?"

She moved out a little from the edge of the doorhole, pushing a hand through her hair. Like a bewildered child she said, "I'm not sure of anything." Matt knew then it was shock made her seem so queer.

She put a hand against the wall. "I'm sure he's gone. He got a horse — I heard him leave. Just after the others did."

Matt's muscles loosened a little. Pace would want a horse on the chance he might have to light out after Matt whom he knew had got hold of one. But the bandit was cagey. Matt didn't recall hearing any horse sounds after the Mexicans. . . .

"I thought everyone had gone," she said. "The peons ran into the woods straight away. I thought I was alone here until I saw you." She stepped out from the wall, slim and tall in the firelight. "What were you looking for?"

"A pistol," Matt said. "Stay back in the sha—"

The vicious crack of a rifle threw its roar through the night. The girl seemed to shiver. He thought she was hit and, piling down, ran to catch her, pulling her bitterly into his

161

arms where she hung almost limp. Then he heard her teeth chatter, saw plaster fall off the wall from the hole where the bullet had buried itself; and he spun her away from him out of the fireglow, and scrabbled round on the ground trying to find the dropped Henry.

Hoofs tore away in the blackness. No chance of catching him now and Matt knew it. The girl had picked herself up and stood rubbing an elbow. Her voice came to him small, sounding lost. "Was it Gurd?"

It could have been. But why kill Carlotta? Matt asked himself, scowling. Pace would have no reason to. Pace would have fired at Matt, not the girl, and Matt hadn't been near enough for error to come into it. That slug had missed only because she'd moved just as it left the rifle. She had bent forward to make out Matt's expression.

In his mind Matt saw Angel fixing to drag her to death with a rope and knew whom he had to reckon with. The man had a better reason now for he'd suppose, with Flores out of the way, the Grant would go to Carlotta. Tara's gun fighter must have let his crew go and cut back to lay in wait for just such an opportunity. Smarting under his setbacks, convinced by vanity he had only to wrap up this spread to get Tara *and* Bellfour, it was exactly the kind of thing he would try. He would never expect the Mexicans to carry on a scrap without someone to fight for.

Matt understood what he had to do. Though he'd have given his right arm, pretty near, to avoid it, he knew he'd have to go back to Bellfour. He hadn't had much time to think about the law, what with Tara and Pace and now this Grant business; but he thought about it plenty as he stood raking the shadows. He had the strongest disinclination to go one step nearer Bellfour than he was. He wanted to get on this horse and split the breeze for far places, but somebody had to throw a scare into that bunch. The girl would never be safe until someone put Angel in the bottom of a ditch.

Carlotta wasn't looking at him hatefully now. He was unable to decide quite how she did look, but he got the impression she was about to come up with the end of her string. He found something unutterably lonely in the way she stood staring off into the night. He pushed El Tosco's reins into her hands, said, "Hold him," and veered off through the darkness for a check of the place, needing to make sure Pace had really gone.

When Matt came back without having

sighted him she was standing as he had left her, still hanging onto the leathers, not turning or speaking even when he retrieved them. But as he swung up she said, "Will you be back?"

He thought about that, wanting to tell her not to count on it but saying instead "Probably," though he had no intention of coming back if he could get clear. He wrenched El Tosco's head around. He had never been able to talk well with a woman. Now he was leaving another one, and he was stuffed with words that might better have been said.

Bellfour, when Matt sighted it, had but one lamp still showing. He'd wasted a couple of hours pawing around through black brush to come up on the place without using the draw. He was being crazy enough without giving them more of an edge than he had to and that draw, he was sure, would be heavily picketed. He'd come down through yucca and a sward of drought-stunted greasewood and watched the yard bleakly for an interminable half hour before he would believe he could approach without detection. And this knowledge, when he admitted it, only made him more distrustful. Except for that one green square of lamplit window he would have sworn the place was deserted.

It smelled like a trap. All those pens and only two horses showing, both asleep on their feet.

He thinned his lips and scanned the layout once more and pushed the black horse into motion. The light was in the house in what he figured must be Tara's office. She wouldn't be working on the books this late. She must be talking with Angel, probably getting his report and likely laying plans for pushing their grab at the Grant to a successful conclusion.

He gave the bunkhouse a wide berth and cut into the yard between the barn and what he judged to be the hoofshaper's hangout, keeping well away from those two corralled horses. He left El Tosco on dropped reins about six strides from the kitchen door which was on the east side of the house and not in sight of the other buildings. He warily tried the door and found as expected he could get in by this means without any trouble. The trouble, he reckoned, would come when he found them.

The thought dried his throat, but there was no good chewing it over. There were too many ifs any way a man eyed it.

With bunched muscles Matt thumbed the latch and, lifting the door to prevent any drag, eased it open. Nothing happened. No one waited inside with drawn gun to cut loose at him. The kitchen was dark as a pile of stacked stove lids and quiet as a tomb.

When he got hold of his breath he felt his way to the hall and eyed the sliver of light leaking over a doorsill. He caught no sound of voices and stood a while, thinking. But thought was no good to him now. In close quarters this rifle wasn't likely to be either, but he kept hold of it and, grimly ready as he could make it, stepped down the hall and threw open the door.

When the Bellfour crew went tearing out of the yard with Flores' Mexicans after them, Gurd Pace had no idea where Matt was. He gave Tretisson credit for more sense, however, than to go larruping off into what had all the earmarks of being a well-baited and deadly trap. He didn't for one minute suppose those raiders had been panicked. He didn't suppose, either, that Matt had taken this chance to get clear. The guy was a natural born sucker, a real Honest John who would no more think of saving himself at the expense of a woman than he'd have thought of sticking up Howisgrenn's bank if Gurd hadn't put the notion into his bonnet.

Pace had got a laugh out of that; Tretisson never suspected Harp James, one of his hands, of tipping off the rustlers where and how to do him the most damage. It was Harp who had suggested after Matt's jobbing from Howisgrenn that only a chump would take such a beating when it lay in his power to even the score with the banker. "Why," said Harp James, spreading on the indignation, "I could even dig up a couple or three fellers that would be damn proud to give you a hand — small-spread jaspers that old buzzard has tromped on plenty." And Tretisson had gone for it. Hook, line and sinker.

But he'd begun to show cagey after the job had been pulled — Yavapai's fault for not keeping his hatch closed! But Matt was stuck with it then, tarred with the same brush as the rest of them he thought. What he still didn't know was that Gurd was tied in with the Quitaque Pool about as closely as Howisgrenn, taking a kickback on every ranch busted. Matt didn't know, either, it was the banker himself who'd set up the bank's sacking, fixing it with Gurd beforehand to split the take right down the middle, Howisgrenn guaranteeing them the chance to get clear of town.

No, Gurd wasn't scared Matt would take a pill and hightail it while things stood as they were right now. There was this soft streak in him, this compulsion for responsibility whether the thing in hand was of his making or not. He would never pull out while he thought the girl needed him.

Reassured by this conviction Pace found and saddled a horse for himself. One thing, by God, you had to say for old Flores, he did himself proud when it came to good mounts. Solid Barb, like you couldn't hardly find no more, crossed on top Steeldust mares out of Texas.

He peered around for Carlotta but in this dark failed to notice her. Not that he gave a damn where she was, really, except as an anchor to hold onto Matt for him. As a person she didn't exist for Pace any more than her hired hands who were wholly expendable. It was Matt that Gurd had his mind on. He might be a chump, but he was showing more nerve than anyone had looked for. Him hiding that swag could play hell with this deal.

Pace climbed into the saddle, then sat there.

After all, dough was dough. What did Gurd owe the Pool? When you came right down to it, there was a heap of things a man could do with that mazuma besides turning back half of it to that sanctimonious banker.

The bandit, darkly grinning, reached a

hand down, tightening the cinch. With a hundred grand a man could go a long ways. If he could get through Bellfour and past the bluffs of the Llano Estacados a man could thumb his nose at the whole goddamn push!

This Tretisson was the only fly in the gravy, and Gurd, by God, knew how to take care of him.

Matt felt like a fool bursting into that room crouched over a rifle and nobody there but Tara with her hair down. And it wasn't an office — he was in the girl's bedroom. He felt the heat crowding into his cheeks as she stared back at him. She was in some kind of loose wrapper with a brush in her hand and a mirror behind her that showed Matt just how damn foolish he did look.

"Wouldn't a pistol be more convenient?" she said. She stared up at him whitely, not embarrassed or frightened. A redheaded woman bitterly angry. She let him know it. "Whom did you think you would find in here anyway?"

He turned angry himself. "By God! You can sit there brushing your hair with people dead and dying all over hell's kitchen! What kind of woman are you?"

She looked at him a long time without

speaking. Then she put down the brush, got a colt .45 from a drawer and held it out to him, butt forward. He found himself taking it, shifting the rifle into the crook of his arm.

"Trouble sure follows you around like a dog." She pushed the hair off her neck. "What's that rag on your head for?" She took a deep breath. "All right, go ahead. Let's have the whole story."

"Where's that gun fighter?"

"By your face you know more about it than I do. He hasn't been around since the middle of the afternoon."

"Where's your crew?"

"Same answer. Only men I can account for are those in the bunkhouse too hurt to ride. Now let's have it," she said grimly.

The only thing he kept back was the part about Carlotta tearing up the quitclaim. When he mentioned Flores' death something stirred back of her eyes and they got darker, brighter some way. When he was done she got up and walked over to the window. Running up the shade she stared into the night. She came back to say quietly, "I don't suppose you'll believe it, but I had nothing to do with that."

"You're paying them," he said, and saw her wince.

Her mouth tightened. Perhaps she was

remembering the shirt, as Matt was. *First Scurlock,* he thought, *and now the whole Flores tribe.* How many others must be offered up to the twisted reasoning of this woman's greed before somebody took a gun to her?

The ungiving look was back on her face, and raw fury burned out of the stare she put on him. Matt had no way of knowing this anger stemmed directly from his own expectation of finding Angel here in the house with her. But, seeing it, he said, "Get rid of them — all of them!" voice sharply intolerant.

"It's too late," she whispered, face crumpling — "I can't."

"You won't be dealing," Matt warned, "with a bunch of scared peons. You'll have me to account to, and —"

"Get out of here!" Tara said huskily. Her eyes flashed wildly, hunting something to hurl at him.

"You'll do it," Matt said. "The law in these parts will jump through hoops for you. Use it — clean those gun rowdies out of here. Give her back that land Angel stole from her father. Square up for the stock you've killed."

He had never seen her cheeks so white, her eyes so dark, so round, so . . . so frantic.

He didn't try to hide his contempt. His voice struck at her harshly. "Haul your conscience out into the light and take a good look at it."

He wheeled to leave and she cried, "Don't go —" but he kept right on turning, striding into the hall.

She sprang after him. "Damn you! I'll bring the law in! I'll —"

His head jerked around at the window she'd uncovered facing onto the yard. She heard the hoofs then and knew by the fierce, raking stab of his eyes he was remembering back, imagining this to be another of her traps. "Matt — wait! They can't know you're here." She said desperately, "I'll go out. . . ."

He looked minded to strike her. "I've had about all your help I can stomach." He thrust the sixshooter into his belt, levered a shell into the chamber of the Henry and quickly moved out of sight. A board creaked somewhere and then he was gone.

15

Far away at the Capital, on the night Flores died, Phoeneas Minch watched the Governor return to his desk and sit down, a slenderly elegant pink-cheeked man with a white mustache. Born under the canvas of a Red River cart, raised in a brothel, one of the most impressive scoundrels ever to rape the public trust, the man was beginning to show his age. New lines showed deeply around his nose and mouth, and he looked as near whipped as Minch, his attorney-general, had ever seen him.

Minch cleared his throat. "Another courier from Muleshoe?"

The Governor nodded.

"Pool wants action?"

"They've gone over our heads; this wasn't from the Pool. It's direct from the U.S. Marshal's office."

Minch softly whistled. "But I thought —"

"You thought, as I did, that when we offered the Pool certain privileges in this territory in exchange for those miserable blocks of stock, all we'd ever be expected officially to do was sit back and clip coupons. We were wrong," the Governor said bitterly. "They want that fool caught — in fact, they want the whole bunch caught!"

"They've asked for cooperation?"

"Asked! They're demanding it!" The Governor tugged at his collar. "They claim the gang is holed up someplace down in the Bellfour country. If our sheriff doesn't take prompt action they're going to send in some deputy marshals."

"Good Lord!" Minch exclaimed.

"Yes. Exactly."

Minch's color had changed to a look of oiled putty. "Any government snooping down there now would ruin us. Bellfour —"

"I know. We've got twenty-four hours to produce the men or their bodies."

"They put it that strong?"

The Governor said testily, "They've given us twenty-four hours. The Pool figures a wink is as good as a gun. They don't want any court stuff, they want them wiped out."

"But those marshals —"

"A bluff," the Governor snarled, "and we can't afford to call it!"

It was cooler now, a chilling damp was in the air. From where he'd anchored the horse Matt could not see into the yard. He could guess pretty well what was happening. All the hoof sound had quit like a yell cut short by somebody's hand.

Matt stood completely still beside the horse, listening to the heavy jerky pound of his heart, catching presently the mutter of a dozen held-down voices. The crew was back. And just as obviously aware of his recent presence in Tara's bedroom.

Sweat moved itchily under Matt's shirt. "She's put out the light!"

"He can only go north or south," someone said. "We've got him."

Matt, swinging into the saddle, had no intention of running. He had come after Angel. Maybe now he could get the job done.

They were starting to move again. Matt waited no longer but put the horse around the house. The light was still poor, but it was strengthening rapidly. They didn't have any trouble seeing that Henry repeater. "That's right," Matt told them. "Stay just like you are and we will get along fine. My business is with Angel. Angel," he called, "step out where I can see you."

Nobody made any visible movement. "What's the matter," Matt said, "is he bashful?"

A damp wind flowed out of the mouth of the draw. Some of the nearer hills began to take shape like smudges from charcoal beyond the roofs of the buildings. Matt felt time begin to squeeze his gut again. He was in a bad spot if they'd put guards out. He said, "What do I have to do to get a rise from that blowhard?" and one of them said sullenly, "He ain't here, fella."

Something went out of Matt then and the

cold lump began to grow again in his stomach. He saw now that in this crew he had a bear by the tail, and while he was trying to think of how to let go of it he heard a door open and the sound of someone's boots moving over the gallery's floor planks. He didn't dare take his eyes off the crew.

Sweat slicked its feel across the slant of his temples, crept out on the skin underneath his shirt. He ached to push back the hat and let the damp air soothe the throb of that bullet gash. He was certain it was Tara walking over those boards. He needed to know what she was up to, but he already knew what would happen if, even for an instant, he removed his attention.

Angered by his mind's confusion, by the dull weight of physical weariness, he was tempted to cut loose with the rifle, almost willing to trade his life for the privilege. That bunch deserved this and more, yet he knew he could not do it.

The bootsteps stopped, behind and a little to one side of him. Tara said, "Put up those horses and go to your quarters. At once! Do you hear?"

Nobody moved. The man who had answered Matt finally spoke, looking small around the mouth in this fast-brightening light. "Get away from him."

A stillness piled up with a wildness beneath that was like a copper wire being tugged in two directions. "Do what he told you," Matt growled.

"On Bellfour," she answered stubbornly, "I give the orders."   ·

The man who had spoken before spat derisively. "If you want to get killed stay right there and keep givin' them."

The voice of Juke said from the side of the bunkhouse, perhaps twenty strides removed from the crew, "If there's to be any killin', I'll do it. Ride out, man."

"I'm not through yet," Matt said. "It's time this outfit was told a few truths. You're not going to grab the Miranda Grant. It's not going to be put out of business either. The Grant's *my* ranch now —"

"Man, ride out!" Juke snarled.

There was little else Matt could do. He wrenched the black's head around and rode toward the draw.

In that quarter mile full daylight came although the sun hadn't yet got above the bluff when El Tosco took him into the depression. There was brush along its sides, greasewood and lesser growth. There was no sound behind. The way he was feeling he'd have welcomed pursuit.

If he was bitter, fed up, he reckoned he had a right to be. If he had met Angel he might have made the man drag iron and taken care, at any rate, of whatever he owed Don Felipe's memory. If he could have run off that crew, Bellfour would have been finished. Nothing he had tried had done a particle of good.

In the strictest sense of the term, this draw Matt had come into was more in the nature of a pass or notch than a catch-hole for runoffs. Where the sides of it began to pinch in and climb he ran into fog, belly high on the horse. All the rock above his head was damply beaded with this moisture. The sour smell of wet earth and dripping brush grew rankly pungent. Impatient to be out of it, reminded of how easily he might be bottled in this slot, it was all he could manage to keep El Tosco at a walk. But he knew any semblance of fright would bring them after him, and he was cool enough now to see how little chance he'd have. He might outrun them and still be caught for they would know every crack and crevice of this region, and he could not count on Juke to help again. Only Tara, putting herself so close to Matt, had caused the man to take a hand.

So Matt had come full circle, and once

again Tara Dow had saved him. No need to ask himself why. She was bound to use him. Determined, in spite of hell or high water, to have her goddamn way! The time to pull out of this deal was right now. This was his chance and it might be the last one; and the only place Pace wouldn't look for him was town.

He climbed out of the thinning brush and fog and saw the bright blades of sun cutting up through the tops of the taller pines. He put the horse into timber, still climbing, continuing south but bearing more to the east, wanting, if it were possible, to bypass the sheep and the men with Lágrimas who would be looking after them.

The troubles of this land did not come from sheep. Or cattle. From water, even — or the lack of it. Trouble came from the hands of men who could not be satisfied with what they had. It had ever been so, Matt Tretisson reflected, and he saw no likelihood of any imminent change. Only when it came to the day of their dying were all men truly equal, brothers under the skin.

In thirty minutes he reached a kind of spur or broken shelf which took him out of the heavier growth into more open country, carrying him north into the bright slant of sun. The trees fell away and a spine of rock

179

thinly covered with earth took him higher through steadily wilder landscape to a region of huge tumbled rocks from which he saw, far below, the roofs of Flores' headquarters.

He saw no sign of life down there and pressed on, anxious now to line out for town, thinking ahead to the dangers it might hold for him, the possibility of running into people he had known; not too likely perhaps but steeped in peril nevertheless. He was not particularly concerned with any descriptions which may have been circulated. He didn't think he would show much in common with those, being differently garbed and riding a horse that belonged around here, not to mention the whiskers he had grown these last days.

He took off his hat and removed the rag Carlotta had used to staunch the flow of blood from his wound, but he did not throw the rag away. He cut more to the east again and caught the leap and rush of powerful water a good several minutes ahead of actually sighting it. When he did reach the creek he was dismayed by the look of it. Rains higher up had brought it out of its banks, a churning howling race of brown water tearing new channels through brush and rocks. It took him and the horse the best part of an hour to find a place where they would stand any chance at all of getting over it. Even then El Tosco had to be repeatedly urged before he would consent to stick so much as one foot in. He whirled back out, loudly snorting and shaking his head.

A quarter of an hour later Matt found a better place, wider and shallower, and the horse, wildly plunging, finally took him across. Matt had no idea where he was by this time, but he figured town must be northeast of him somewhere. A mighty sweep of country lay spread out below him and nothing in sight that he could use to get his bearings. Some of this, east of him, must obviously be in Texas. He pushed on north but six miles later was forced to turn east, an impassable gorge blocking all travel northward.

Now the nature of the terrain forced him back on the creek and he got down and wet the rag and washed the caked blood out of his hair. He let El Tosco drink before he got back into the saddle. He made three more attempts to push north during the morning, wholly without success. He shot a rabbit near eleven and cooked it over a fire of dead sticks while El Tosco browsed in the shade of piñons.

A little past noon they made another dip

into the north and were able this time to continue, unblocked by any prank of geology. They dropped down off the slopes through second-growth woods, mostly blackjack, rough on man and horse but passable. The country became more gently rolling, and three miles later they came across a dusty wagon road. Here Matt pulled up to sit scowling, unaccountably reluctant to put the mark of El Tosco's hoofs there for anyone to read. It was Pace he was thinking of.

He turned the black horse around and rode back into the brush, confident the road would take him to the county seat — Tara's town, Sixshooter Siding, which some were already beginning to call Tucumcari. He was suddenly afraid of that road, and pushed west through the brush onto higher ground and looked again into the north, seeing a far-flung slant of buttes and bluffs, pale blue and beige with darker streaks of green that from this vantage seemed almost brown. Juniper, mesquite and scrub cedars fringed the skyline with the high slants of the hills reaching into the blue.

East, perhaps ten miles away, he saw a ranch headquarters, the red sides of outbuildings crouched below the white shine of a silo and, off to one side, the glimmer of dug tanks. It was while he was bringing his glance back to the gray ribbon of road that he discovered the riders.

There were eight of them, sending out tiny slivers of silver light as they jostled their horses into a huddle directly facing a broad-shouldered man on a big chestnut gelding. Matt watched them sitting in their saddles there, talking, and no one had to tell him that these were star packers.

They were pretty near two hundred yards away, and he knew they had not yet discovered him. Not wanting them to, he sat frozen in place. Now another horseman appeared, waving his hat, his mount throwing up whirling spurts of dust as it closed the distance and was pulled up beside them. Something flashed in the hills beyond the red painted buildings and the broad-shouldered man answered this with a mirror. Matt knew then he was stopped. He didn't need to see the flashes which presently blossomed in the west. The law had sewed all that north country up with a cordon of scouts. There'd be no breaking through.

16

It was an hour past dark when Matt sighted

183

the lamps of the Flores ranch through a tangle of cedar. Had he come direct from his view of the posse he could have been here hours ago; but he had still thought, slipping away undiscovered, to cut past and get around them. And because he didn't want El Tosco's tracks on the road, he had run west into the hills he'd spent most of that morning trying to get out of. Foolish and useless, a sad waste of time.

And now the distant east was closed too.

From where he stood in his stirrups high above the trees he could see, far off, a long line of glittering dots pinpointing a blackness that was probably Texas. Like jewels these were — like a rope of diamonds couched in dark velvet. A pretty dream; but in cold hard truth he knew these for watch-fires. When, in his head, he toted up a quick reckoning of what it must cost to mobilize and maintain such a force out here at the tail end of nowhere, he had some idea of what he was up against. The long arm of the law was about to catch up with him.

He found it hard to believe he had achieved such importance. Finally shaking his head he put the black horse in motion. He took a deal of care coming off that slope, having no wish to attract a sudden burst of blue whistlers since he had no way of knowing what may have happened down below there. The big trouble with Angel was the fellow's lack of patience.

Tara's face ran through the mixed-up notions prodding Matt, and Carlotta's angry voice, lifting abruptly out of the house, sent him tight-lipped toward the veranda.

On the north-south road three miles above Grant headquarters, much nearer than where Matt had earlier caught his glimpse of them, the integration squad of the law's gigantic posse found themselves with a knotty problem which had not been anticipated. Their supreme commander, Sheriff Raines himself, had stepped into the brush to relieve himself and vanished as though from the face of the earth.

Filled with snarls and fury, Angel, at Bell-four, in complete disregard of his employer's emphatic orders, was heading for the bunkhouse. Tara, shaking and frantic, was climbing out of a bedroom window. Juke, alert in the background as always, was slipping a saddled horse out of the corral. The heavy gloom of full dark was making this easier than he had looked for when the horse stepped into an empty pail.

In the palace of the old Spanish governors,

at Santa Fe, Phoeneas Minch was staring white-faced at a dispatch just torn open. It had come from the U. S. Marshal at Austin and advised that "the affairs and whole background of a combine known as the Quitaque Pool are in process of being thoroughly investigated. Any aid you can render. . . ."

Lágrimas, in the hills with the sheep, was squatting by his blankets under an ancient mesquite chewing smoking tobacco when Eladio came out of the dark with his stick. "I have been thinking," said the herder, "and it comes to me that if the old man dies —"

"You speak of the *patrón?*" Lágrimas inquired.

"Yes. If Don Felipe dies," Eladio said with great patience, "what will become of his people?"

"There will always be sheep and someone must care for them."

"And what of the girl?"

"She will marry the gringo —"

"*Chingao!* Him of the two *pistolas,* you mean?"

"No, the other. He is a man, that one."

"They are not friends, those two. He may need help. Should we not go down there?"

186

"To what purpose? These things, Eladio, resolve themselves. I, too, have not been without thought. One who steps in the way of a bullet is soon dead."

"Well, that is true. You think we should not go down then?"

"Each man to his job. Our work is with the sheep."

Ten strides from the veranda at Grant headquarters Matt pulled the horse up and got wooden-legged out of the saddle. A confusion of light from open door and broken windows spilled deep into the black of the yard, revealing the brush-clawed look of him as he stood, bone weary, seeing no one, hearing only the brittle run of the girl's voice. He was reaching to rip the rifle out of its scabbard when rough hands laid hold of him. It took a moment for Matt to clear his mind of the surprise. By then it was too late. With his arms twisted up behind him they were shoving him toward the door's bright oblong, across the clatterous boards of the veranda.

Anger bolted savagely through him, and he tried in a fury to trip the man on his right. Almost tearing his arm off, the man on the left yanked him back, swearing, striking him. The next thing he knew they were in the house and he was blinking, half blind, at the face of Gurd Pace. The bandit had one hip on the table. "Welcome home," he said with a bright shine of teeth. He had a gun in one fist, finger looped around the trigger.

Matt twisted his head to find who had hold of him, and Harp James, clean shaved and broadly grinning, put pressure into the twist of Matt's arm while Wishbone's rabbity face showed its buck teeth in a windy grunt as he reached across Matt to wrench the sixshooter out of Matt's holster. He wasn't quite able to make it without letting loose of Matt, and Yavapai, built like a snake on stilts, limped across from a corner in his black Texas hat, flipped the gun free and shoved it into his belt. He packed his own at his groin in a brass-studded holster, and he had a cat's yellow eyes in his wedge-shaped face.

Scorn moved across the bitter curl of Matt's mouth. He knew them all, for these were the men he had once shared his blankets with — the very rustlers who had robbed him, though he had not suspected this when Harp James introduced them as small-spread friends Howisgrenn's bank had put out of business. They were Gurd's men, all of them, the infamous "Pace gang" who had helped him stick up the Muleshoe Bank.

"Are you still running loose?" he said; and Yavapai, snarling, stepped in cocking a fist.

"That'll keep," Pace drawled; and it was then Matt noticed the strangers, the two badge-packers, roped hand and foot to their chairs along with Carlotta. One was the broad-shouldered fellow he had seen at the road block.

"Pace," Matt said, "your goose is cooked. A dog couldn't get out of this country right now. They must have called out the troops, maybe Indian trackers —"

"I'll git out all right when I'm ready," Pace said. He jerked a thumb at the broad-shouldered man and grinned derisively. "There's the sheriff. They ain't goin' to be doing very much without him around to lay out the orders."

"That's where you're wrong," the sheriff smiled. "They've got their orders."

The bandit's eyes turned ugly. He took his hip off the table. He walked over to the man, yanked his shirttail out and, ripping off a fistfull, rammed it into the sheriff's mouth. Then he hit the man in the face, so hard it sent the chair crashing over. "Cut that other cutie loose," he growled at Yavapai, and then sent Wishbone off to find the man a mount. Wishbone, with his run-over boots suddenly stopped on the veranda, put his puff-cheeked face back in through the door. "How about Tretisson's nag?"

"Sure," Pace said. "Matt ain't goin' no-place." He hauled around to eye the perspiring deputy. "You bust back to that posse, mister, quick as you can git there. Tell 'em the orders has been changed. Tell 'em, by God, if they come one inch closer — or so much as one shot is fired into this camp — I'm goin' to cut this John Law in two with a pistol. You got that?"

"Yes sir."

"See you remember it," the bandit scowled, looking half minded to rough him up to make sure of it. "Tell 'em I'll be takin' him with me, and I'll be keepin' him with me as long as I need 'im. What happens after that'll depend on the kind of coopera-tion I git. Now haul outa here."

He gave the man a shove toward the door and fastened his slate-colored eyes on Matt. Tretisson hardly noticed, just having stumbled over a considerably startling fact. Tara Dow, back at Bellfour before she'd come out to block their fire on the gallery, had called him Matt. Not Calico but *Matt.*

Harp James, cruelly twisting the arm he had hold of, jerked Matt out of the shocked

190

fog of this discovery. "The boss asked you a question, Tretisson."

Matt heard the ground break under a fast-starting horse, heard hoofs go tearing across the yard. He saw the involuntary protest of the sheriff's broad shoulders where they sagged against the lashings anchoring him in the knocked-over chair.

"He heard me," Pace said. "He knows what I'm after." Wishbone came in trailing cold air and whacked dust out of his clothes with his hat.

Matt said, "That hundred grand's going back where it came from."

Pace stared, prodding a back tooth with a sharpened match. Spitting the snagged particle of food from his mouth he pointed the match stick at Wishbone. "Take hold of him."

As Wishbone moved in, Matt stamped on James' foot and almost got loose of him. Wishbone hauled back a boot and kicked Matt in the belly. When this jerked his head down Harp brought him up with a hook to the jaw. Matt didn't quite go limp, but he was not among those present for a couple of splinter-edged minutes. When his eyes began to swim back into focus, Pace said: "Where is it?"

"Go to hell," Matt said thickly.

"Always the sucker," Pace sneered. "Don't you know it was Howisgrenn set this whole deal up? It was him killed that clerk after we'd run off your cattle. You ain't hurtin' —"

"I sure as hell ain't helping you!"

Pace nodded to Yavapai. The gangling hardcase stepped in and cracked Matt across the face while the other two held him. Left then right, then left again, hard punishing blows that bounced Matt around like a penful of broncs.

Blood ran out of his smashed nose. Yavapai hit him again. Carlotta screamed. Wishbone and James lurched sideways with Matt's weight. He spat out a couple of teeth when he came to and Pace motioned Yavapai out of the way. "You goin' to spill now?"

Matt grinned through cracked lips.

Pace said, "By God, I'll make you talk!" and whipping the match across his pants he clapped the blazing end to Matt's cheek. Matt's whiskers went up like a celluloid collar. He had lost his hat and flame ran through his hair with a *whoosh*. The room stank of singed flesh and Matt, nearly out of his mind with the pain, heard Carlotta mumbling Hail Marys in Spanish.

Pace caught a grip in the front of Matt's shirt. "You figurin' to have me try somethin' else?"

A framed picture came off the wall with a crash. Pace, whirling, saw Yavapai stagger. The fellow's mouth stretched wide in a yell that wouldn't come. Pace saw the dark hole suddenly open in his forehead as Yavapai fell in a curling drop to the floor. The wild sound of rifles ran through the house then.

17

Tara hadn't the slightest intention of bringing the law onto any part of this range when she had told Matt she would. That had been spite talk sprung out of resentment. She'd been bitterly riled, this vexation still seething when she'd come onto the gallery to find him facing the pack of mongrels Angel, one by one, had added to the payroll over her protests. But mixed with the anger then had been fright, and it was fright which had moved her to stand beside Tretisson.

She was more frightened now as she rode through the night on the horse Juke had given his life to secure for her. She had known terror when the horse, stumbling into that bucket, had brought guns to barking all over the yard; But Juke had managed, though staggering, to bring the horse round the house and to thrust the reins in her hands. "Ride," Juke cried — "I'll hold them off," and he had, the only man left who had been with her father.

All the arrogance and pride she had erected to hide her helplessness was gone, scratched away by panic fear. All the makeshift expedients she had tried in desperation had failed as she should have known they would, even the ruse of Scurlock's shirt which she'd thought — if Matt didn't do it — would force the range boss in self-defense to kill or drive Angel away. Now Scurlock was dead, and Flores and Juke. All her fears had converged in the inescapable conviction that only the sheriff — the law she had been too mixed up to call on — could stop this. The man was like a mad dog, and the boldly grinning look of him, encountered at every turn these last weeks, gave new strength to her flight, a new awareness to purpose.

This was something she should have done months ago; there was no middle ground, you couldn't compromise with wrongness. A person had to take a stand — she could see this now. Responsibility was the burden of all, a public cross each soul must bear. The alternative was chaos.

She urged the horse to greater speed,

tore over a crest and saw the eyes of a thousand fires. They ringed the night like fallen stars. . . .

It was the sound of rifles that galvanized Pace, the jeering rasp of Angel's yell rolling over the yard that drove him, snarling, to slam Matt over the head with a gun barrel. "Git to the windows!" he shoved Wishbone wickedly. All Matt's unconscious weight fell on James who cursed and let go of him, spinning to dive for the room's second window as Pace with two shots put out both the lamps. The racket was bedlam, and when Harp managed a look into the outside night there was nothing to shoot at that a pistol could reach. Bellfour had learned its lesson; they were keeping well back in the brush and letting slugs do their work for them.

A great crashing and banging came from the kitchen and, irascibly swearing, Pace slammed off down the hall. Wishbone, squatted under one of the windows, dragged a sleeve across the gleam of his face and orally wished he had never left Texas. "Them stinkers is like t' make a job of this, Harp."

"Yeah," Harp said, "must be a dozen of 'em out there. Sift around a little and see if there's a window — Hey! Where the hell are you?"

Getting no reply, he crawled across the floor and felt around in the gloom that over here was like spilled ink. He did not find Wishbone — nor any trace of him. He wouldn't believe it, then his gut began to pinch and he grew further alarmed when he noticed how quiet the inside of the house was. Not a gun being fired except by Bell-four.

He became concerned with the state of his health. He forgot Matt entirely and again looked outside, jerking away when a slug bit into the casing beside him. He dropped back on the floor with the clothes damp all over him and began to move crab-like through the gloom toward the hall.

Someone out there was using a Sharps. Every time it went off it was like a can-nonball hitting the side of the house. He got into the hall which held no smell of powder — there ought to have been if Pace had been firing.

This bothered Harp, though not as much straight away as his thoughts about Wish-bone. There were only two doors to this stuffed sausage of a room, the one Harp was crouched in and the one giving onto that bullet-riddled veranda. No one but a dimwit would have gone out there, and where the hell else could Wishbone have got to if he hadn't crawled into this goddamn hall? "Why," Harp said under his breath, "it's the only place he *could* go!" But he didn't believe it. He'd have heard him go past.

"God damn!" he growled nervously. Staring into the murk he tried to think what to do. He knew what he wanted to do but if he tried and Pace caught him he might just as well cut his throat and be done with it.

He listened to the slugs steadily breaking things up. Dust got into his nose and he strangled a sneeze. "Jesus!" he whimpered. With extreme reluctance he set off down the hall.

It was like crawling into the gullet of a cow. Every third time his right knee touched the floor he hung fire and said "Gurd . . ." in a kind of parched whisper. He was a man cut adrift in the teeth of hell.

In the front room Matt, on the floor where Harp had dropped him, seemed to have been listening for ages to the crash of Bell-four lead. He heard someone crawl past him in the direction of the hall and knew his gun was in Yavapai's belt and that Yavapai wasn't six feet away from him.

Might as well have been six miles, he thought — the torture of knowing wouldn't have been so fierce then. The whole gang had been in this room when Pace struck him, and he had no idea where the other pair were. If he moved and they were here. . . . He got away from that thought hurriedly and had a vision of Carlotta tied lifeless in the chair.

Cold sweat broke through the pores of Matt's skin and itched unbearably at every gather. His burned face throbbed, his head hurt too. Every tunneling slug seemed to scream through his skull, and if he didn't get out of here one of them might find him.

Twisting his jaw he found the vague bulk of the sheriff's tipped over chair. He saw the girl's shape plainer, but he couldn't make out any movement. He couldn't make out her face although the dim gray blob of it was toward him. If she were still alive and conscious she ought to be showing some sign of life. Perhaps, he thought, she was frightened. He was pretty damn scared himself, come to that.

He stood it so long as he could and then, very carefully, drew up one leg. Someone said *"Gurd"* in a barely audible mutter. Matt thought it came from the hall, and he held his breath. He put some weight on his hands then and turned himself over. A slug laid its breeze against the side of his neck. Two more whispered *cousin,* but no gun went off inside the house. He tried to catch some suggestion of breathing, but all he was sure of was the rasp of his own. A gun spoke suddenly from one of the back rooms and Harp yelled, "Christ! That's me, Gurd — watch it!"

Matt didn't listen to Pace's answering snarl. He moved while he was covered by it, lifting his pistol from Yavapai's belt. Then he got the man's own gun from the brass-studded holster and moved to the girl, hearing the whine of Harp's voice. Matt touched her face and it was warm. He pushed Yavapai's pistol into his waistband and, sheathing his own, reached down for the ropes. "I'm all right," she breathed up at him. "Free the sheriff — he'll help you."

Matt considered, grimly viewing his chances, finding no hope whatever he did. He bent over the ropes again, located the knots, silently cursing their tightness. It was while he was trying to get one of the ends loose that he realized Bellfour had about quit their firing. He was reasonably certain they hadn't run out of cartridges. Reconnoitering probably, scouting to see if they'd got the job done.

Not much help there. Angel wasn't the kind to put great value on hostages. But it might just be, if he could get these damned knots loose. . . .

Alarm rang through Matt's mind. The whole house was too suddenly quiet — as if every timber were listening. He raked a glance toward the hall, seeing nothing. What were that pair in the back up to now? Had they heard him? Had Pace remembered he wasn't tied?

He pried at the knots again, got one of them started. He worked feverishly at it, his fingers all thumbs, cold shivers stalking up and down the ridge of his spine. Sweat stung his eyes, and as he shook his head to clear them some fragment of scuffed sound jerked his stare up, stopped his breathing. He couldn't tell if it were inside or out. He gave the ropes a final tug and felt the knot unravel.

He turned and dropped Yavapai's gun in her lap, turned again and, suddenly convinced the sound had been in the house, moved away from her, drawing the other gun. This was the .45 Tara had given him.

He had a moment of black suspicion, wondering if it would fire. Pace said from deep back in the hall, "Go out through the front and we'll git them between us."

After his pair of scouts had departed to try and find out how things were at the house, Angel — inordinately pleased with himself — called up three others, the toughest of the lot, gun-notchers all. Making sure they had plenty of cartridges, he told them his plan and passed the word back for the rest of the crew to hold up their fire. The scouts he wrote off before they'd got out of sight, not believing, as they did, this deal was wrapped up. This Flores place — infinitely more durable than Angel's patience — had been built to withstand seige.

Sufferance had never been Angel's chief virtue, and temper was prodding him too in this instance. He could not afford to wait; he had enough to live down as things stood right now. Word of his two previous setbacks here must already have gnawed at his record's advantage. To be stood off again might encourage their enemies to where they'd gang up and tear Bellfour into doll-rags. Some of this bunch were ready to bolt now.

He would hamstring these Mexicans and Calico with them! All it would cost were those two chowderheads he'd sent off to play Bridger and Fremont. When the Flores crowd jumped them he would know where to shoot.

"Let's go," he told his three hardcases. "We're doing this afoot. Keep your eyes skinned for flashes and then pour it into them."

Matt didn't know, hearing the approach of those boots, if it were Wishbone coming up the hall or Harp James. Acting wholly on instinct he reached back to touch the girl with a cautioning hand, then got down on the floor, disposing himself as nearly as might be in the fashion they had left him — with one unobservable difference. The fist doubled under him clenched the butt of a pistol.

The boots quit the hall and with an awkward stealth came into the room, pausing uncertainly just out of Matt's reach as though the man looked around or perhaps peered through a window. Matt could hear the diffident rasp of his breathing. Suppose this jigger took it into his head to go over there and try Carlotta's bonds? Matt would have to squeeze trigger — he could never in this world grab a hold in time to throttle him.

The floor creaked under the man's shifting weight. A great drop of sweat gathered itself and hung quivering on the point of

Matt's nose. The boots moved again, doorward now. He heard their hollow groans cross the boards of the veranda. Stiffly rising he vaguely saw the man's shape crouched vulture-like over the dark gleam of a rifle. This must, he thought irrelevantly, have been the Henry off his saddle which one of them, giving Matt's horse to that deputy, had apparently left outside the door.

The man was Harp James.

Matt heard the girl's ropes softly slide to the floor. He was beside her at once. With his mouth against her ear he warned, "Don't move the chair — get to work on him where he is." He heard the swish of her skirts as she dropped onto her knees. "Knife in my right front pants pocket," the sheriff murmured. Matt found it. He put it into the girl's hand and pulled off his boots while she was cutting the officer loose. "Give him Yavapai's gun," Matt said, and stepped carefully around the fireplace. There was nobody on the veranda now — no one in sight, at any rate, from this angle. Feeling as though he'd been dragged through a knothole Matt padded over to the farther window.

No sign of Harp. But off to the right out there, near the brush, a stick snapped loudly. Three guns went off in a racket of echoes, one slug punching through the slack of Matt's shirt as he dropped. On hands and knees he moved across to the door, coming onto his feet to peer over the wreck of the veranda railing.

There was breathing behind him. The sheriff said carefully, "Better give them time to show." The girl's hand touched Matt's elbow. Matt said without moving, "Any horses around?"

"Gurd's bunch left theirs in the stable," Carlotta whispered.

Matt moved onto the veranda. The boards felt cold under his bootless feet. He moved into the darkness of the yard, intently listening.

"But we can't," the deputy told Tara. "All you say may be true, but there's nothing we can do about it now. They've got the sheriff over there. I ain't gonna be responsible for gettin' him killed."

"What about Tretisson? What about that girl?"

The man shook his head stubbornly. "She'll have to take her chances. Tretisson's a murderer —"

The sheriff nudged Matt, jerked his head toward the right.

Off there where it looked darkest, by a

204

corner of the house, there seemed to be a suggestion of movement. Matt stared until his eyes felt like they'd pull from his face. He heard Carlotta's strained breathing, the thud of his own crazy heart. "Get back," he mouthed; and the sheriff said against the side of his head, "Look left of the stables."

Matt's swiveling glance picked up a shape, bent low, barely moving, obviously bound for the black hole of the runway. "Hang onto Carlotta."

He moved on bare feet to cut the man off, got as far as the horse trough when guns ripped the night in five places, two slugs pounding hollowly through the end of the planks. Matt ran for the stables. A rifle's sharp voice jumped out of the gloom and Matt saw Harp James dive into the runway. Three pistols cracked spitefully. He saw Harp go down.

Near the house another gun spoke and someone thrashed in the brush, yelling stridently. The sheriff called something that was drowned in the uproar. Matt fired at the flashes, still running, saw two shapes break across the yard. The sheriff got into it, staggering one of them. The other collapsed as though cut off at the knees.

Matt pulled up at one side of the doorhole, knowing without seeing him there was someone inside. It was something felt, an acute awareness.

He twisted his head and found Carlotta beside him. The sheriff came up, peering back across a shoulder. And over by the house a gun threw its wink of light twice against the blackness. Inside the stables something clattered; a rat struck the floor and scampered away trailing a drift of stirred dust. Deep in the gloom a horse stamped nervously. Matt edged into the place, feeling his way with an outstretched foot, sliding it on until his toes touched Harp's body.

He dropped into a squat and felt around for the rifle without discovering it. Carlotta whimpered, but this Matt ignored, listening and waiting, probing the darkness left and right. A horse grunted somewhere and moved the hind half of him, a hip scraping the partition as he sidled around.

Matt straightened, tipping his gun up, every sense reaching out to catch and define any shift of shadows. Farther back a horse snorted and something of about the weight of a cartridge bounced off a wall and fell into the dirt.

The sheriff, outside, said clearly, "Keep your eyes peeled — I'll come in through the back," and crunched away while still talking. Up ahead a tiny blotch of paleness fractionally moved. He fired twice. The stables roared.

The clamor faded. The stench of powder swirled around him. Someone sighed and something fell.

"Tretisson!" Carlotta cried.

Matt stood still, coldly waiting with lifted pistol. A dim flutter of hoofs drifted down through the timber, was lost, came again, swelling louder, building into the throb of a great body of onrushing horsemen.

There was a nearer churning of hoofs and the sheriff, back of the stables, cried: "Stop!" and emptied his pistol. The back door was yanked open. "That bunch from Bellfour has — You in there, Tretisson?"

Matt, lowering the pistol, finally stirred. "I'm here," he said and, remembering the lantern, found and lit it, lifting it over his head. He saw the sheriff. Lowering it he stepped over there, stood looking down at the man he had shot. He bent over Angel, took hold of him and, letting him go, slowly straightened.

"You know, of course," the sheriff said, "I'll have to arrest you."

Matt, nodding, passed over his empty gun. feeling a kind of weird disappointment whᵣ this failed to produce the relief he'd pected. The sheriff was looking oddly embarrassed as though hardly knowing what to do with the weapon. The whole thing, Matt thought, was faintly ridiculous, the sheriff standing there with two empty pistols. But there was something . . . Matt said suddenly, "What happened to Pace?"

"Nothing happened to Pace," Pace said, coming in behind the white face of Carlotta, whom he steered by the arm he held twisted in back of her. "Drop those guns, mister."

There was nothing the sheriff could do but obey. Pace, showing his teeth, spun Carlotta away from him, so hard she crashed into a stanchion, half falling. Matt flung the lantern. Pace, ducking, fired, but Matt was already dropping. He caught a flash of bare leg as the lantern slammed bluely into a wall and went out. He grabbed the pearl-handled sixshooter out of Angel's dead hand, hit the ground dizzily rolling and came up, driving two rounds into the pattern of Pace's fire.

Matt was shocked, almost incredulous, to find he had not been hit by any of it. Crouched there, locked in the grip of this, he heard the reedy guttering of the bandit's breath. "God, man," the sheriff cried — "don't let him die! You'll have no witness. . . ."

It was Sheriff Raines himself who found

208

and lighted what was left of the lantern, holding it up in shaking hands. All the glass was broken out of it, the frame was twisted, but nobody noticed. Both Matt's shots had found Pace and the haft of a knife was sticking out of his back. He was dead and the yard was suddenly clamorous with horsemen.

It was a pretty whipped-out-looking group of people who gathered a half hour later in the wrecked front room of the old Flores ranch house. Lamplight showed the grease on Matt's burns. He had described for the sheriff where the bank loot was buried, had heard from him how the Bellfour crew had glommed onto their horses and dug for the blue. "What's left of that bunch," Raines said with satisfaction, "won't be stopping this side of Colorado."

He smiled sympathetically at Tara and Carlotta. "Now that you've agreed, Miss Dow, on behalf of your syndicate to make restitution, it kind of seems like to me this country ought to get along."

They had all heard from the sheriff's chief deputy of Tara's ride to get help for the Grant, and of how he had refused because of Raines' plight to move until they'd heard the guns. "When I heard that firin'," he said again, "I knowed damn well holdin' back wouldn't help him. If they was goin' to knock him off he'd be stiff sure by that time."

The sheriff nodded. "Well," he told Matt, "I'll do all I can to help you. A jury's hard to figure, but I'm frank to say that without what you done this whole deal could of wound up a mighty heap different. I'll testify to what Pace said about that clerk and Howisgrenn's —"

A strangled hollow-sounding cough cut him off and all eyes slanched around to watch a black rain of soot mound up and scatter out over the hearth of the fireplace. Raines' deputy jumped up and snatched out his firearm. "Come down outa that!" he growled, looking fierce, and Wishbone — the last of Pace's gang — still coughing, wriggled out of the chimney.

He was a sight. But quick as he got back enough breath to fetch words with: "I'll blab," he gasped hoarsely — "I'll give you enough dirt on Gurd an' that banker to. . . . Hell's fire! whaddaya think I clumb up that blamed chimney fer? To git outa Pace's way — that's why, an' I tell you —"

"Get it all down in writing and get his John Henry on it," Raines told the deputy. "We ain't promising him a thing, but if what he says gets Tretisson off. . . ." He looked around after Tara who had got up and gone out. "Hmph," he said, thoughtful. "Well —" to the deputy, "after you get it all down, take him over to the bunkhouse with the rest of them prisoners. No use in us pullin' out of here before daylight."

It appeared as though Tretisson might wish to say something, but when the sheriff gave him the eye Matt settled back glumly. "Hell," Raines grinned, "go ahead if that's what's itching you. I reckon she'll keep you occupied till I get done with the rest of this."